Taking Comfort

R.N. MORRIS

© Roger Morris 2006.

Roger Morris has asserted his rights under the Copyright, Design and Patents Act, 1988, to be identified as the author of this work.

First published in 2006 by Macmillan New Writing.

This edition published in 2020 by Sharpe Books.

For Rachel, who has waited for this

CONTENTS

1. The Di Beradino classic
2. The Snoopy ring binder
3. The Twirl mug
4. The Yves-rocher Yria Extreme Comfort Lipstick bronze
5. Pringle socks
6. The GN 2100 Microboom Mono Headset
7. The Unifor i Satelliti S200
8. The Prêt à Manger All Day Breakfast
9. The Benjys napkin
10. The Evian Natural Spring Water 0.75l Nomad bottle
11. The Jammy Dodger
12. The Nobo Brainstormer Flipchart Pad
13. The Ideal-Standard Space btw wc
14. The Hugo Woman fragrance
15. The Mulholland Brothers Messenger Bag
16. The pint of London Pride
17. The Sabatier Au Carbone 8 inch Carbon Steel Chef's Knife
18. Sloggi Basic midi briefs
19. Blue Hawk Plaster Coving 127x2000mm
20. The Xpelair integral timer remote switch operated extract fan
21. The Philips AJ3120 radio alarm clock
22. The Nike Air Zoom Elite running shoes
23. The Flexi Classic 1 small dog 5m retractable dog lead
24. Whole Earth Organic Corn Flakes
25. The Tetley teabag
26. The IBM ThinkVision L170P flat panel monitor
27. The Montblanc Meisterstück Le Grand fountain pen

28. The Unifor Progetto 25 screen system and the TAG Heuer Kirium Ti5 Men's Chronograph
29. The Securicor security box
30. The generic handkerchief
31. The 5 Star Document Wallet
32. The Tracy Island movie tie-in toy
33. The Jonelle Egyptian Bath Sheet
34. The Cobra Premium Beers
35. The Eurocopter EC135 Advanced Police Helicopter
36. The Martyn Gerrard window
37. The Marvelon contraceptive pill
38. The Barbour Harris Tweed jacket
39. The Sony KV-20FV10 20" WEGA TV
40. The BODYARMOUR UK Police Concealable Body Armour vest
41. The Initial 2-Fold Hand Towel
42. The Bic biro
43. The Google search engine
44. The Yves-rocher Yria Lip Contour Pencil brun
45. The BT Synergy 3105 cordless digital phone
46. The Ikea Grundtal dish drainer
47. The Starbucks Coffee cardboard cup
48. The Pizza Hut pizza delivery trestle
49. The Nokia 6610i mobile phone
50. The Arofol Plus self seal postal bag
51. The L.K. Bennett kitten heels
52. The Faithfull Steel Shaft Claw Hammer 16oz
53. The Nissan Bluebird 2.0GS
54. The Yale P1037 door chain
55. The i'coo Platon three wheeler

LONDON, 2005

1. The Di Beradino classic

In his hand, you have to imagine how it feels, the Di Beradino classic briefcase. It all starts with that feeling in his hand.

Classic styled briefcase from Di Beradino hand crafted in beautiful vegetable tanned leather with satin finished solid brass fittings

The whole focus of his being is in the grip of his hand around that hard leather handle, in the way the seam stubs into the underbellies of his fingers, in the swing of the handle in its solid brass satin finished fittings. In the sense he has of its contents and how they influence the swing and how that swing uplifts him.

Robust stitching and lined with a cotton material Flapover conceals triple sectioned interior plus pockets on front Size 44 x 33 x 14cm

He is a marketing man. He can appreciate the abrupt punctuation-free poetry of that copy. And is perhaps more willing than most to allow it to influence him. Vegetable tanned leather. How could he resist it?

The case is a present from Julia. That she was able to choose it for him, that she's willing to spend the two hundred pounds plus on him, two hundred pounds out of her teacher's salary, that she did this for him. It's proof of something. It reaffirms his faith in her, in both of them. It is as if she has presented him with a leather-goods interpretation of himself. This is you, it says. I know you, I understand you, she's saying.

He grips the handle and feels the swing.

2. The Snoopy ring binder

He feels a brim of sweat insinuate itself between fingers and handle. He is focused on that film, on how it lends a granular quality to the beautiful vegetable tanned leather of the handle. Is that the salt? he wonders. He wants to wash his hands but he's standing on the down escalator in Highgate tube station. Suddenly the air around him is grainy.

He watches the theatre ads pass by, shows he will never see, and the vitamin ads and the cereal bar ads. He wonders at the significance of them. Not what are they saying to him, but what do they say about him? Why are they placed here for him to see? What are the demographic assumptions? Shows he will never see, vitamins he will never take, cereal bars he will never eat. And the high energy drinks ads. He feels complicated by the ads, sad and slightly resentful, the way he feels after watching certain American TV series, the ones that Julia likes. He feels that the ads have placed him in a false position. That he must now go to the shows, take the vitamins, eat the cereal bars, drink the high energy drinks or run the risk of being superfluous. And he is willing to do it, he feels he must do it, because doing it is what the world expects of him.

But he does not feel any of this very strongly and he doesn't allow it to depress him.

It's ridiculous, of course. You must understand he realises this. More than that, he enjoys it, the absurdity of it. He's as close to laughing out loud as any man standing on a down escalator in a busy tube station can be.

Entering the platform, he changes hands, sharing the privilege of carrying the Di Beradino. He thinks about the miracle of her buying him the case, presenting it to him this morning in honour of his first day.

His last job was Charing Cross Branch. This job is Bank Branch. It will take some effort of will to remember.

He flexes the free hand, giving the sweat some air, and checks the display. First train up, Morden Via Charing Cross, two minutes. Next Bank train, four minutes. Not so bad. He doesn't want to be late on his first day.

He realises he should be thinking about that, focusing on that, but instead he's concentrating on the feel of his fresh hand around the handle, living there, enjoying for a moment the pleasure of the Di Beradino classic, weighing its cargoes, emotional and otherwise.

The case contains the comb bound acetate covered *Welcome to Diamond Life* document, his current paperback and a banana. He felt odd putting the banana in there but this is his work case, a working case. It must contain the things he needs it to contain. Otherwise what's the point?

Normally he would take a couple of bananas so in a sense the single banana could be thought of as a concession.

He realises he is not nervous about his new job at all. He is eager for it, cannot wait to claim it. He is impatient. Does not want to linger on this platform. If he is nervous about anything, he is nervous about the people on the platform. There is a flow that carries him to the far end, away from the entrance.

He looks at women. This is something he does. He looks at and assesses their sexual attributes. He hopes he does it in a way they do not notice but cannot be sure. Once a girl in a low-cut top, a plump girl, a girl as plump as fruit, a girl who seemed to be making a display of her breasts, the skin was there for all to see – once such a woman turned away from him in a tube compartment. They were standing near the door at the end of the compartment and she turned her back on him for the whole of the journey. She must have caught him looking at them, at the taut-pored skin of them, but, hell, he was reading his current paperback and any glance he had made in the direction of her fruit-plump breasts was furtive in the extreme. So furtive he had not even caught himself doing it. But she must have sensed it, or assumed it, which annoyed him if it was merely an assumption on her part. Just because he was a man he must be looking at her breasts! It was galling. But of course it wasn't overly galling. He was, after all, looking at her breasts.

He's doing it now, looking at them, the women, at their sexual attributes, breasts and bums and thighs and, in the case of those that are wearing trousers, there, that place, the apex. Great word, he thinks. He is a marketing man, remember. But it's quite hateful, he hates himself but cannot stop.

And now there is a new place, he has noticed, that women reveal. The belly, the flash of flesh between the buckle of their belts and the bottom of their tops. It is an important place, a section of female rotundity. It leads down to there, the apex. A giddy camber, it seems to invite the sliding of a tensed palm down. And they display it. He does not make them do this. They do it willingly. They are either fools or they know full well what they are about. And he is expected to walk past these glimpsing bellies and not look. He is not allowed to look. He knows he must not look. And yet, he is supposed to find a way too. It is part of the game, the crux of it. They want him to look, so they can be disgusted at him, at his weakness.

The women he looks at in this way, all women to some extent, he wonders if any one of them reciprocates his glance with a glance of exactly equal meaning, equally assessing, equally laden with a quality of hopeless, pointless desire. (If only they could appreciate the poignancy of that glance!) He doubts it. He is not one of those men that women look at. Few men are, he thinks.

The platforms at Highgate are longer than they need to be, longer than the trains. There is an empty space at the end of the platform. The trains always pull past it. He was caught out once. Never again.

He's nearing the invisible cordon that marks the beginning of the no-go area when he sees her. Or rather that is the moment he is conscious of seeing her. Something chimes, something that makes him think he knew about her all along. She makes him nervous. There is something familiar and precise about the nervousness she inspires. She is the focus of all the anxieties he feels towards everyone, towards the very idea of people, or at least those people on the platform. She almost scares him.

She's young, a student. Japanese, he thinks. He's not very good at making racial distinctions but he thinks he can tell Japanese from Chinese, for example. She has a large flat face, round like a plate. Not pretty, but fascinating. Appalling almost, in the sense that there is something in that face that you do not want to see. A blankness. But also an intensity. A fixity of purpose. Despair. This is despair, he thinks. She's hugging a Snoopy ring binder to her chest, covering her breasts, which he guesses are tiny. And it's the Snoopy ring binder that conBarrys him she's Japanese. He has the sense that they go for that sort of thing. And she's dancing. Yes, dancing. Or that's how it seems when he first is aware of seeing her. She's moving with measured steps in a circular sweep, a repeated movement, advancing, retreating, sidling, circling. Her partner in this dance is the platform guard. Standard-issue London Underground guard, royal blue shirt, peaked cap, running to fat. They are face to face. And he moves with her. When she goes to the side, he goes to the side. When she backs off, he backs off. When she steps forward, he steps forward. And all this is strange and worrying to see. Rob cannot make sense of it. All he can do is grip the handle of the Di Beradino classic.

Then he realises what's going on. He's blocking her. The guard is blocking her. She's trying to get to the edge of the platform and the guard is trying to stop her. They do not say a word to each other. Maybe she doesn't speak English. Or maybe there are no words that can be said. All the guard can do is position himself between this girl and her intent. He is whispering into his walkie-talkie.

Then something happens, something terrible happens. The overhead sign reads TRAIN APPROACHING. The air begins to rumble. The light in the tunnel enlarges. He can feel the vibrations underfoot. And it's now, at the worst possible moment, that the stationmaster, or some other blue-shirted London Underground official, comes striding onto the platform. He calls out to his colleague. The platform guard looks up. And in the moment of his distraction, she gives him the slip.

As the train bursts out of the tunnel she leaps off the edge of the platform. Arms and legs akimbo. And Rob is horrified that he has time to think of the word akimbo, a word he has always enjoyed, that it should occur to him now. It is as if she is trying to scatter herself to the ends of the earth, the shape she makes. It is more than akimbo. Akimbo doesn't do it justice. The blunt front of the train innocently proclaiming MORDEN VIA CH+ gathers her up and carries her off without ceremony or resonance, with just a kind of defeated crumpling. He hears, or thinks he hears, over and above the frozen squeal of the brakes, the brisk thud of the collision, the screams around him, something that he takes to be the last breath expelled from her body.

And now he sees two men comforting each other. The platform guard, the girl's last dance partner, is windmilling his arms and wailing. The sound of his cries is hurk hurk hurk. The stationmaster is trying to slow the movement of his arms, is attempting soothing strokes that don't strike home. He's batting at the other man's despair. He realises the only thing he can do is hug him, pull him to him, and hold on to him. He does not question the impulse. The stationmaster is taller than the platform guard. He holds the other man's head to his shoulder. The hurk hurk hurk is muffled now and the station master's shirt is quickly drenched with tears.

No one else there has that licence, to choose another to give and receive comfort. The rest of them, all the others there on that platform remain only strangers. They look to each other, they search each other's faces. But it cannot go beyond that.

And then he sees it. It's there on the platform she dropped it the Snoopy ring binder. And in the shrieking chaos, Rob feels the need to retrieve it. He would never have guessed that he would do this, dip onto one knee and in a fluid movement scoop it up. That he would have the presence of mind or the need.

The vinyl touch of it, there is comfort in the vinyl touch of it. He thinks he understands. Why she was holding on to it, holding on to it for dear life. It is cushioned and textured, stippled, a texture like skin, only without pores, this skin. It is hermetic, sealed. It has a slight sheen. There is comfort in the touch of it, even in the touch of the rigid moulded seam. The colours comfort. The white of the background. The yellow of Snoopy. Snoopy comforts. He has never really understood Snoopy until now. The black lines. He runs his fingers over it expecting the different colours to feel different. There are only three colours. White, yellow, black. The simplicity and boldness of the colours comfort. He is not disappointed. The different colours feel different. The black lines feel raised. They come out to meet his touch. He imagines them on a molecular scale, as massive ridges. The yellow is raised too, though not as much as the black. It's like a gentle plateau.

He thinks he understands why she was holding on to it and why she had to drop it. Why she could not take it with her.

He looks around to see if he has been seen. But no, everyone is absorbed in their own horror. Or if he has been seen, it is without comprehension. This is a moment when nothing can make sense.

He has the ring binder tucked under his elbow now and is fumbling with the satin finished solid brass clasp. For now that he has it, the Snoopy ring binder, there is only one place it can go. Inside the Di Beradino classic, between the comb bound acetate covered *Welcome to Diamond Life* document and his current paperback.

3. The Twirl mug

Where do they come from, she thinks, the mugs? And why is purple the colour of milk chocolate?

She has in her hand the Twirl mug. She always seeks it out. She realises it is not a classy mug. Perhaps she feels sorry for it. Or more likely it is an act of defiance.

Did people bring them in, previous employees?

A curling sheet of A4 sellotaped to the wall reads, PLEASE LEAVE THIS KITCHEN IN THE STATE YOU WOULD WISH TO FIND IT.

She is not afraid of anyone and never consciously waits for the kitchen to be empty before she goes in. There is nothing anyone here could say to her that would unnerve her. Rather it is the other way round. She has power over some of them, some of the men. That's what it gives you. That is the reward. Power. She senses it in their nervous shifting eyes, the fear.

She realises that part of the attraction of the Twirl mug is the destructive relationship between boiling water and milk chocolate. It's a fantasy but always in the instant before pouring the water over the tea bag (Sandra only ever drinks tea) she imagines that the cup is actually made of chocolate. She can even picture it melting. And it is that idea that makes her seek out the Twirl mug.

It is not a classy mug but few of them are. Perhaps they should do something about the mugs. Perhaps she should suggest it. But that would mean losing the Twirl mug.

The previous notice had read, PLEASE LEAVE THE KITCHEN IN THE STATE YOU FIND IT. But that didn't work. All too often people found it in a disgusting state. It was she who had suggested the new wording. Soon after, she was moved to marketing.

Everything is connected.

The new wording has improved things.

While she waits for the kettle to boil she opens the fridge. There is milk. That is a bonus. There is not always milk.

Especially not on Mondays. Still you have to check the date and sniff it.

As the kettle climaxes one of them comes in, one of the men she has power over. Tony. Ironically, he is her boss. But that is his lookout. He once, she once, they once. But now all that is behind them. Now there is only the nervous shifting fear in his eyes. And her quiet power.

They nod to each other, like mates but not.

But she is not wholly easy about this one. She is reluctant to exercise her power too blatantly. The ultimate power is his, she knows this. He is the one who can fire her. So she finds a way to appease him.

She remembers.

Coffee?

Ta.

She finds him a nice mug, a classy one. Habitat.

One sugar?

Go on then.

You can have Canderel if you like.

Do me a favour.

You lost weight? she asks.

You think so?

Yeah.

He pulls himself up with a dishevelled shrug, tipping it off with a happy little perk of the eyebrows. She's made his day and she knows it.

She thinks back to he once she once they once. And nearly shakes her head at the absurdity of it. But there is nothing for either of them to regret. Nothing for either of them to discuss. But there are rules in not discussing it.

New boy's late, says Tony as he watches her stir away the instant coffee granules.

Oh yeah. He starts today, doesn't he. I'd forgotten. What's he like?

Tony's lip flinch is non-committal. He says only, Late.

Not good.

Not on your first day.

Maybe he's had a change of heart. Cold feet?

He gives a squeaking chuckle at her thought. And adds: What? Change his mind about working in this place?

Sometimes, she says. She doesn't smile but something in her voice suggests amusement.

What? He's picked up on it, the something in her voice.

She won't answer, is too busy squeezing flavour from the tea bag.

He opens the bin for her. They are like any couple. They are close.

But it will never happen again. She knows it. She wonders if she will have to spell it out for him, hopes not.

Don't forget this afternoon, he says.

I hadn't.

She takes her Twirl mug back to her desk.

4. The Yves-rocher Yria Extreme Comfort Lipstick bronze

She checks her smile in the mirror of her compact. And rolls her lips around the freshly-applied Yves-rocher Yria Extreme Comfort Lipstick bronze. She is the public face of the company.

This is the great comfort lipstick! Its fine film texture glides over your lips for a sensation of absolute comfort and impeccable hold. Its radiant colours will dress your smile with colour and femininity. Its vitamin formula leaves lips smooth, supple and superb!

She finds the taste of it comforting too.

Her line is perfect. The line she drew with the Yves-rocher Yria Lip Contour Pencil brun.

Donna is a dab hand at outlining the shape of her smile.

She takes her job seriously and is rewarded for doing so. If this company has got one thing right it is to cherish their Senior Reception Manager, though she could do without that Senior, thank you very much. The rewards go some way towards compensating her for the things she has missed out on. It's no one's fault she missed out on these things. Least of all the company's.

The building has an atrium and in the middle of the atrium is a tree. It's nice and airy around the tree. The atrium is four storeys high. And there's a glass roof and the light floods through the glass roof in a way that is almost religious. The upper floors enclose the atrium with glass walled galleries. People look down at the tree and from time to time Donna looks up at the people. Occasionally someone will wave to her, cheerily. It's very calming to look at the tree and to allow the space around it to work on you. Best seat in the building she has, wouldn't swap it for any other. And the tree symbolises something. Life, growth, hope. Roots. The tree has real roots that go through the floor of the atrium.

There have been men along the way. Some of them were bastards and some of them were married to other women. Not always the same men, the bastards and the other women's husbands.

The tree is not an oak tree, though you might expect it, this being a life assurance company, a financial institution in other words. The tiny acorn sentiment. Perhaps someone thought that was too obvious.

She has no problem with the kind of clothes they expect her to wear. They are the clothes she would choose anyway, given the money, which they do. Smart. Extremely smart. Austerely smart.

But she has a nice smile. She knows that. She has always been told that. She has staked her life on the niceness of her smile. It is something. It is not nothing. The younger ones like her. They ask her along on their girls' nights out. She's like an older sister to them. It's only the men, boys really, they are little more than boys, who call her Ann Robinson. And even that she doesn't mind. She can take a joke. She knows how to laugh. Joins in. Calls them the weakest link.

She would never have Botox, though in a way she is like an actress, a celebrity, on show, her looks her livelihood. So who could blame her? But it never works, does it. She's happy with her hydrating products.

There are no tears, there is no secret sorrow eating away at her soul in the middle of the night. She looks in the mirror and checks her smile. She looks at the tree and sees something reflected there too.

Roots. There is something to be said for roots, no matter where you plant them.

She puts away the compact, some sixth sense guiding her, she has been in this job long enough to know when to put away the compact, when the revolving door will revolve, she always senses it before it happens.

And sure enough the revolving door revolves and a man comes in, thirtyish, mid-thirties maybe, sort of mildly good-looking, but something about his face mocks any kind of judgment along those lines. For his face is grim. She cannot take her eyes off his face. She does not want to look there, but she cannot take her eyes off him. There is something there that reminds her of all she has missed out on, of the men along the way, the bastards and the married ones, of how old she has become sitting in front of that tree, something that mocks her compensations, her clothing allowance, her hydrating beauty products, her airy atrium and her tree roots. Something against which even Yves-rocher Yria Extreme Comfort Lipstick bronze cannot comfort her. She shivers, she actually shivers, looking at his face.

His hand is shaking as he lays it on the reception. His face is waxy white. He looks as if he has been crying or might cry any moment.

I'm Rob Saunders, he says. I start work today. In the Marketing Department.

She tries to smile. She really does try. She tries to offer him her smile. She feels he needs it. They both need for her to smile.

I'm late, I know, I...

He looks away from her. He lifts his other hand to his face. He's holding a briefcase. It's a nice briefcase, she thinks. Leather, tan. Expensive looking. She feels better seeing the briefcase.

I'll call Tony, she says.

He nods. He's looking at the tree.

5. Pringle socks

The socks are important but let's not dwell on them. The point is everything is important. Even socks. And these are real Pringle socks, not the cheap imitation crap you can get off the street traders. He's onto them.

The socks are important. The tie's important. The shirt's important. The suit's fucking important. And let's not forget the shoes. The shoes are important.

If you must know:

Socks, Pringle.

Tie, Liberty.

Shirt, Thomas Pink.

Suit, suit, the fucking suit is Paul Smith, of course.

The shoes, Dolce & Gabbana.

It's not that he's into labels. It's just that he's into quality. It's an inner thing. *He* knows. That's enough. No one else needs to know.

Trolleys, Marks & Spencer. Of course. Always. He is loyal. Even if it is only to an idea. Or maybe it's ironic. He can't decide, doesn't feel he has to.

He used to wear cheap socks but the big toe always went through. It's not worth it. In the end, it's a false economy.

He's looking down from the atrium. He sees the tree, he sees Donna, he sees the new boy.

What fucking time does he call this?

He almost rubs his hands with glee.

Oh dear oh dear oh dear.

It gives him such pleasure to form those words, even if only in his head. It gives him such pleasure to have the upper hand.

Into the lift and he's staring at his own smoky reflection and he is suddenly no longer enjoying himself. He could be happy if he never had to look himself in the mirror. He tries to smarten up, brushes the flakes from his shoulders and lapels. Since when did he have dandruff? He tightens the tie. Tony tightens the tie. There is not time to retie it but it's all wrong. The ends are wrong. How did it get like this?

He needs a haircut, he realises. He's let it go too long again. Lunchtime. Maybe. If there's time.

Long hair on a receding forehead. It's a mess. He looks a clown, he knows it.

Thank Christ for the Pringle socks. The Pringle socks, unseen, remain perfect.

The lift door opens and he's crossing the floor of the atrium, hand extended, calling out:

Rob!

The hand shake.

He cannot resist a jibe: We thought you weren't coming. Thought you'd changed your mind.

No, I. It wasn't that.

The missus didn't want to let you go, is that it?

I… there was trouble on the line.

Where do you come from?

I get the tube from Highgate.

Northern Line.

That's right.

Northern Line's crap.

Yes. It can be.

We thought you'd got cold feet.

I'm sorry. It really was the journey from hell. It won't happen again.

Tony nods. He looks at Rob and nods.

Are you all right? he says. He doesn't want to but he can't help himself.

I'm all right, Rob answers. Sure.

Come on then. We've lost enough time already.

And Tony turns away from Rob and is quiet as he leads him into the lift. He has seen something in Rob's face that he cannot bear to dwell on.

6. The GN 2100 Microboom Mono Headset

This is not something he will admit. If you put it to him he will deny it. But he likes the way it makes him feel. The headset. The GN2100 Microboom Mono Headset.

The excellent sound quality of the GN2100 Microboom Mono surpasses anything you might have experienced before in headset technology.

The headset plugs into his computer, interfaces with the network. He's talking to a customer. He can call up the database on the screen, on the seventeen inch OptiPlex flat screen. He calls up the name, the details. Policy number, name, postcode is all he needs. Check the first line of the address. He has it all there. The details, the policies, the works. He can do this.

The headset plugs into his computer, but on another level, on a deeper level, this level is the level of the soul, the level at which the soul vibrates, at this level the headset plugs into his childhood.

The attractive and unique three-in-one design takes personal comfort to a new level, letting you choose the most comfortable wearing style; either a headband, SureFit earhook or adjustable FlexLoop.

He's a boy again, back in the bottom bunk, and the bottom bunk is a craft, a space craft, it has a bubble hood, and he commands it with his eyes, with his eyes in the dark, in the darkness of space, between the asteroids.

And he is safe in the bottom bunk. And he is safe in the craft that he commands with his eyes. And he is safe with the GN 2100 Microboom Mono Headset cradling his head.

He calls it the twenty one hundred.

You could call it the two one hundred. Or the two thousand one hundred. Or the two one double zero. But he calls it the twenty one hundred and he feels sure that he is right to call it that.

He wears it headband style. He is man enough to wear his headset headband style.

Cup one ear. Touch your ear, or anywhere on your head. Understand the comfort, the real physical comfort that comes from cradling, cupping, touching an ear or any part of your head. Just to touch your hair, just to brush it lightly, accidentally almost.

That's what he gets from the GN2100 Microboom Mono Headset.

The computer tells him he has a call. He hears it in the headset, the throbbing pulse of incoming. And it's there on the screen. INCOMING CALL.

Hello, you're through to Michael. Do you have a policy number for me?

It's about the insurance.

I see. But, uh, I do need a policy number, if you have it. You are an existing customer?

My husband used to deal with it all.

Could you give me your name?

Emily Green. Mrs Emily Green.

Postcode?

Sorry?

Your postcode. Could you give me your postcode, please?

HA2 5QS.

House number?

It's a maisonette. We have the upstairs.

I see. But it does have a number?

42B.

OK. I have your details on screen now. How can I help you?

He can do this. He can talk to the woman, he can hear the quake and quiver of age in her voice. He can feel the fear welling in her voice. She is not a suspicious woman, he senses. She is trusting. He can feel the trust in her voice. He wants to help her. He has her details on the screen. She is not a nasty woman, he feels. She is not bitter. She is sad. He feels the sadness in her voice. And he has her details on the screen. He wants to help her. He can help her. He has her details on the screen. This is his job. He can do it.

But she is not there. She has gone. He cannot help her if she is not there.

Emily?

She comes back to him. Her fear, her trust and how he imagines her face, something birdlike in her expression, he imagines. All this comes back to him with her voice.

My husband died, you see, she says.

And he doesn't want this. He cannot help her with this.

He looks away from the screen, knowing full well that he will not find the answer on the screen. He looks across the floor of Inbound Calls. Square after square of tight-weave compact-piled carpet tile. Hard-wearing, doesn't show the dirt. It is a system, a floor-covering system. As one wears out in the centre, you swap it for one at the periphery. It makes sense. Not his choice, of course, not down to him, but how he would do it if it was his choice. It is not a comfortable floor. The dun squares hold no comfort. But they do not show the dirt and that is more important in a work environment.

He sees that fat guy from marketing come in and remembers. Today is the day he's agreed to have a new guy sit in on his calls. And sure enough there's a new guy with the fat guy from marketing, with Tony Dawson, is his name. The guy with him, he knows he is the new guy because it is a face he does not recognise. And there is something in the face that he does not want to recognise, something in the face he turns from.

He is glad of the GN 2100 Microboom Mono Headset cradling his head.

She is still there. The details are still there. Hello? Hello? she's saying.

He can do this. He can call up her details on the screen and listen to her saying hello while holding out his hand for Tony from marketing to shake and for the new guy to shake. He can listen to her telling him about her husband dying while nodding to Tony from marketing as he plugs another headset into his computer. He can watch Tony from marketing hand the second headset to the new guy while glancing at her details on the screen. He can hear Tony tell the new guy to pull up a pew, while listening to the fear in her voice.

He can do all this.

I'll leave you in Michael's capable hands, says Tony. He claps his hands together once and rubs the palms together, as though this is a wonderful thing he has done, this leaving of a new guy in Michael's capable hands.

Listen and learn, he says and he's on his way back across the carpet tiled floor of Inbound Calls.

It's all a bit of a shock really. My husband died, you see.

She's still there, a voice in the GN 2100 Microboom Mono Headset. Her details are still on the screen.

Last week it was, she says.

I'm sorry.

He raises his eyebrows to the new guy. Can you believe this? is the meaning imbued in the raising of his eyebrows. He knows that meaning is there because he put it there. But the new guy is out of it.

And he used to deal with it all, you see.

She's still there.

And what exactly is the problem, Emily?

He knows her name is Emily because it's there on the screen. That's what the screen is for. He doesn't have to remember. He's not expected to remember. The screen remembers.

Well, it's leaking. The roof. It started leaking. It started when he was in hospital. I couldn't bother him with it. Obviously. And then he died. So I didn't know what to do. My husband used to deal with all that, you see. Anyhow Carla downstairs said I could get it on the insurance. We've been with Diamond Life for fifty years, you know.

That's very uh, wonderful.

He looks back to the new guy. Talk about over his head. Where do they get them from?

Well, I phoned up about it and they've sent me a letter now.

Just give me a moment.

He feels the resisting pressure of the keys under his fingers.

She's fucked.

Look at his face now, the new guy's face now! He can't believe his fucking ears! He doesn't get it. Look at the poor bastard. Better put him out of his misery.

'S'on mute.

He can do that. He can press a key on his computer, two keys actually, hold one, hold control, Ctrl, hold that and press Pause/Break and it switches the phone on mute. He can do this and he can say things like, She's fucked. He can do this. He does it. Often. He loves to do it.

Hold Ctrl, hit Pause/Break and he is back talking to Emily.

I see yes. It's a flat roof. That's right?

That's right, yes, she says, the poor old trusting, fearful, sad and fucked old bitch.

Well, Emily, as it says in the letter we sent you, we don't actually insure flat roofs.

But we paid the premiums. We've been paying the premiums getting on for fifty years.

Unfortunately, it seems your policy was never actually valid. It should never have been approved in the first place.

But you took all that money off us. And you never said.

It's probably because the original policy was set up so long ago. The rules must have changed. You should have been notified.

My husband used to deal with all that.

There isn't really anything we can do to help you in this particular instance. I would suggest that you cancel the policy as soon as possible, as it is…

Hold Ctrl, hit Pause/Break.

Not worth the paper it's fucking written on.

Do it again. Hold Ctrl, hit Pause/Break.

…not appropriate for your property. We don't actually insure flat roof properties. At all. You will have to go to another insurer. Would you like me to cancel the policy for you now?

What about the leak?

As I said, there is nothing the company can do.

So let's wind this up, he thinks. And to show he's thinking it he gives the new guy the winding up sign.

You took all that money off us. For something that was no good.

I will make a note that you are not happy with the policy. If you have a complaint, or comment, or concern, about any aspect of the service you've received, we do have a procedure. There is a form I could send you.

The training helps. He is trained how to react in these circumstances, or similar ones.

It's not right, is it?

There is pleasure in the way the keys resist his fingers, there is pleasure in the way his fingers know where the keys are, there is pleasure in the way he doesn't have to think too hard about the keys or the fingers. He can let them get on with it. Sort it out between themselves. There is pleasure in efficiency. And comfort too.

I've cancelled the policy for you, Emily.

She's gone. Has she gone? It seems she has gone.

Emily?

He treats the new guy to shrug. What else can he do? What can he say? There is nothing that can be said. Only a shrug will do it.

Thank you for your call, Emily.

Ctrl End ends the call.

So, welcome to Diamond Life. How you settling in?

7. The Unifor i Satelliti S200

He is given a desk. A workstation is how Tony describes it. The desk or the workstation or the whatever surprises him. He touches it tentatively as if he suspects they will take it away from him immediately. Or is he just reassuring himself that it is real? He looks to Tony for something. He can tell that Tony, the man who is to be his line manager, does not like looking at him.

The Di Beradino classic slips neatly under. He is reluctant, however, to surrender it.

Tony is explaining about the desk. It is a desk that needs explaining. There are handles you can turn. You can make a section of it go up and down. Turns out you can make the whole thing go up and down. The top, the whole of the top. It adjusts.

i Satelliti S/200. F&L Design

Furniture for the office. Created for a new way of working, capable of interpreting the most complex of problems with simple solutions. Surroundings that are open, light-filled, natural, flexible, functional. Designed through a use of few constructive elements that define spaces, passageways and situations that differ functionally from one another. A unique modular system, that has what it takes to respond to the most widely differing needs. Activities, procedures and duties that coexist in an atmosphere of mutual respect.

Rob is having a hard time making sense of the desk.

It seems very, he says, not finishing his sentence. Wondering what on earth he had it in mind to say.

Tony looks at him for a long time.

Rob rubs his finger along the surface of the desk. At last he manages to say, Smooth.

Yeah, agrees Tony. And solid.

It seems he has said the right thing. Or at least he has not said the wrong thing, which is worse, and what he is afraid of.

Fantastic engineering on these desks, explains Tony. As you can imagine, he adds, they are not cheap. Oh no. But it's important, says Tony, explaining about the desks. These things are important.

Rob frowns. He doesn't feel he really understands. About the desks. About anything.

What things? he asks.

The environment, explains Tony. The working environment. The workplace. If people are comfortable at work, they will be more efficient. That's my argument. The desks were my idea. There was a lot of resistance, as you can imagine. At board level. I had to take it to board level. I had to make a presentation. What's this got to do with you? they said. You're marketing. This isn't marketing. This has got nothing to do with marketing. But everything's connected, is my point. The brand. It's about the brand. The way people feel is the brand.

Right, says Rob.

If people feel right at their workstations. I won't say comfortable. It's not about comfort. Not totally. It's about the brand. It comes across. That's what I said. They bought it. I was fucking amazed.

Yes. It is, says Rob, not finishing his sentence again. He thinks of adding, Amazing. But before he can Tony says,

So a few of us are going down the Feathers this lunchtime.

Rob frowns. None of this makes sense. Is this about the desk? he thinks. Or the brand?

Just a quick one. We have to be back sharpish. Got a meeting I want you to be in on.

Rob nods. He can do this. He can nod.

So do you fancy a quick pint? Get to know the rest of the team?

Ah, the penny drops.

I thought I might just get a sandwich, Rob says, too quickly, he realises. He holds out a hand. It shakes. With the other hand he reaches down and touches the Di Beradino classic. He knows the Snoopy ring binder is there inside it. He wants to stay close to the Snoopy ring binder.

This morning, Rob adds. It is all the explanation he is able to offer.

Forget it, says Tony. But Rob does not know what he is meant to forget.

Forget what?

Being late. It's all right. Just make sure it doesn't happen again.

It won't happen again. There is a questioning tone, a desperation in his voice. Will it?

The idea that it might happen again terrifies him. He touches the Di Beradino classic.

Well, if you change your mind, says Tony, we'll be in the Feathers.

8. The Prêt à Manger All Day Breakfast

He must eat. Whatever happens, whatever will happen, whatever has happened, he must eat.

But the front of the train as it gathered her up. Will he ever be able to take the Charing Cross line again?

It is perhaps a mercy, for him, that her body obscured the driver's face. He thinks it would have been worse to see the driver's face. He thinks he can imagine it but he can't. He hopes to God there was no one driving. But of course there must have been someone.

He knows now that he saw blood. He knows now that blood obscured the driver's face too. That blood was sprayed onto the platform, that it was the hot sprinkle of blood that drew the screams from those nearest. He knows that he felt it on his face. Is the blood still there on his face? he wonders.

He walks. He does not know where he is, has no idea. He finds it hard to remember who he is. Everything has been severed by that blunt front of the train and by the hot spray of blood.

Perhaps he should have gone to the pub. He understands now what Tony was asking of him. It was not to do with whether he wanted to go there. It was not to do with whether he was thirsty. It was nothing to do with beer. It was to do with what was expected of him. It was expected of him. He knows he is adrift, severed from himself. Normally he is so good at knowing what is expected of him.

But he is hungry. He must eat.

There is a Pret. He loves these places. These places afford him deep comfort. Especially in the run up to Christmas. He loves the cinnamon smell. He loves the coffee and cinnamon smell. He loves the piped carols and Bing Crosby and the lilting anonymous jazz. He knows that the sandwiches are overpriced but they are not really overpriced because what you are paying for is the cinnamon smell. He doesn't need to eat the pastries. Just to smell them.

It is all right. It will be all right. The warmth and the smell and the presence of food. This is comforting. This is comfort.

Even the noise in these places is comforting. The ceramic and aluminium reverberations. The shouting of the counter staff, Yes please? Take away? Anything else? Thank you. Next please. Yes, sir. Even the shouting is comforting. The aluminium everywhere is comforting.

And he has the sense that he is not the only one who comes here for comfort.

He sees a girl, a woman, some city girl in a two piece, who seems to look at him. He can almost believe she smiles at him, that there is some interest there. But there is something hard about her face, he thinks. She holds something back. She will always hold something back, he knows. And anyhow, it is all nonsense. She is a stranger in a sandwich shop. Why is he even looking at her? Why is he even thinking this? There is Julia, Julia, remember? he reminds himself.

She who gave him the Di Beradino classic. She who was able to interpret him in leather goods.

He has it in his hand, the Di Beradino classic. He didn't want to leave it under his desk or workstation or whatever. He didn't want to let it out of his sight.

The most comforting sandwich he can think of is the All Day Breakfast. It is not really an all day breakfast because the egg is boiled, hardboiled, and that's not quite right. It should be fried. The yolk should run. At the very least the yolk should run. And yet it works in the sense that it satisfies. It is a deeply satisfying sandwich. It is a simple sandwich yet there is complexity to it.

He has the sense that she is looking at him again, as he weighs the All Day Breakfast in his hand. The packaging, angular, brown, cardboard, pleasantly functional, smart. It feels good in his hand.

She, he notices, is choosing the Pesto Pasta Salad Bowl. Nice.

He saw someone die this morning. He witnessed a terrible violent death. A rip through the fabric of the universe, is the cliché that comes into his mind. He knows it is a cliché but it comforts him. And now, here he is, a few hours later, weighing a sandwich in his hand, thinking idly lustful thoughts about a complete stranger, watching what she chooses out of the corner of his eye. Approving her choice. Wanting to know her. Wanting to fuck her, he realises. For all the hardness of her expression, for all the sense he has that she will hold something back, that he can never know her, perhaps because of all this.

But it is nonsense. It is all nonsense. It is always nonsense.

He feels sick. He cannot eat. Must he eat? He must eat. He must at least buy the sandwich.

He will have a Coke too. He finds the plastic bottles more comforting than the cans.

9. The Benjys napkin

It is not the run up to Christmas. There are no piped carols. It is Spring. It is a pleasant Spring day. The sun is shining. The City is a place of glints and celestial reflections. Clouds expanding in the curvatures of car bonnets. He is hot in his suit jacket.

He has the Di Beradino classic in one hand and the Pret bag in the other.

He walks.

He passes a TV showroom. Every screen has the news on, showing footage of disaster. An earthquake somewhere. He lifts the Di Beradino and hugs it to the chest, mirroring precisely the gesture of the Japanese student, presuming she is Japanese, presuming she is a student. Or rather, was.

The Snoopy ring binder is in there. That is the important thing. That is what he knows.

He walks. He must walk. He must eat. He walks hugging the briefcase, with the Snoopy ring binder inside.

He finds a place, a small square in front of a church. There are two park benches facing one another. There is a couple on one bench. They have sandwiches. Their sandwiches are from Benjys. He can tell this from the napkins and the bags.

He does not know what sandwiches they have. Basic ones. That is Benjys. It is more the basic kind of sandwich. It is the place to go for your basic sandwiches. Your ham and salad. Your cheese and pickle. Your basic egg mayonnaise. But it is also the place to go for hot bacon and egg sandwiches. Real breakfast sandwiches. Hot and freshly cooked, while you wait, in front of you. On a griddle. It is the place to go for hangovers, not to get one, but if you have one. The bacon and egg sandwich will sort you out. With sauce. Brown or red. These are the choices that define us.

He finds it hard to choose.

He takes the other bench, the bench opposite the couple. The Di Beradino classic is on his lap. He wants to look inside it but he must eat too. He knows that he must eat but he is not sure if he will be able to. So much has happened. He saw a girl, eighteen, say, nineteen, twenty at the most, he is not very good at ages, not at the ages of different races. Was she Japanese or Chinese? She could have been Korean or Thai or Taiwanese. It is a question of confidence. The same thing as remembering names or general knowledge. That is to say, he knows really. He is absolutely certain that she was Japanese. He knew the moment he saw her that she was Japanese. It was not the Snoopy ring binder. It is just that we all know these things. The patterns, the facial racial patterns, subconsciously, it does not take much for them to imprint themselves on us. And identifying birds, the different species of birds, and genera of plants. We can all do it. It is there in all of us, the ability. But some people, Rob is one of them, they lack the confidence. To say so, even to themselves. But he knew. He knew immediately she was Japanese. Something else he knew as soon as he saw her. He knew what she was intent on. He knew what she was about. He knew what she was trying to do. He knew that she would do it. He knew. He pretended that he didn't know, pretended that he had no idea, pretended that he did not know the meaning of it, of that dance, the dance with the platform guard. But he knew, immediately or very soon after immediately. And he knew also that she would drop the Snoopy ring binder and he would bend and pick it up and take it away.

And now he sits and sees this couple and they have sandwiches and the sandwiches come from Benjys and the girl is shaking her head and tears are streaming down her face. He sees this and cannot take his eyes off her distress. He realises now that they are not eating the sandwiches, they are picking at them maybe. How often do you see people eat sandwiches by tearing away morsels with their fingers? It is always a sign of something when you see that. He saw that right from the beginning and he knew.

The girl is crying and shaking her head. The guy sits with his head bowed mumbling. The girl's face is glistening red and streaked with tears. In the City of London sunshine her tears glint like the chrome trim of a newly delivered car.

They are not dressed like City types. They are dressed like student types and that makes him nervous. He is wary of student types today.

They're wearing motif T-shirts. His says *The White Stripes* next to a picture of a monkey holding a guitar. Hers shows a yellow hazard sign with a figure struck by lightning and the words DO NOT ANGER THE GODS. The T-shirts are tight on their slim bodies. But their trousers are baggy. Voluminous legs. He loves that word. Just loves the sound of it. And capacious. He always was a sucker for the Latinate word. He strives consciously to keep them out of the marketing documents he writes professionally but he always acknowledges them when they come to mind.

Rob puts the Pret bag next to him on the bench. He opens his briefcase, the Di Beradino classic, and looks inside. The scent of the vegetable tanned leather comes up to comfort. He sees the Snoopy ring binder.

I can't believe it. I can't believe it. I can't believe you'd do this to me.

He hears these words distinctly. The guy is mumbling, head bowed mumbling, but the girl speaks these words clearly. And now she's wiping her eyes with one of the Benjys napkins. There are no crumbs on it because she has not really eaten anything.

We've cleaned up
Sandwich Manufacturer of the Year
Specialist Sandwich Retailer of the Year
Marketeer of the Year
BSA Gold Standard Manufacturer
BSA Gold Standard Retailer
Investor in people
benjys
Less bread
www.benjys-sandwiches.com

She shakes her head and puts the napkin on the Benjys bag. She does not look at the guy. She gets up and runs. She runs. She throws herself into her run and it's like he's watching the Japanese girl again throw herself off the edge of the platform.

There is that same sense he has of a person wanting to be obliterated by a movement.

Somewhere in the world there's been an earthquake. He knows this. He saw the scenes on the muted shopwindow TVs. Thousands, probably, are dead. He does not know, but he supposes so. A terrible event. A country in mourning, somewhere. Which one? Turkey he thinks. But this is worse. To see this girl run. To see her streaked strained face. To see her throw herself into the motion of her distress. And to be reminded.

The guy, the author of her anguish, though who knows, there are always two sides, the guy hunches over. He picks at the sandwiches. But without conviction. He has lost his taste for your basic sandwich. It is not long before he gets up and takes off himself, not running, his step is slow, as though he is tethered by a powerful elastic strap to the bench, to the Benjys sandwiches. He takes off in the opposite direction to the girl.

It is an age before he clears the square and all the time Rob's pulse is thrumming. Because he knows what he will do, what he must do. And he knows he must do it quickly.

He gathers his things, the Di Beradino classic and the Pret bag. He must move fast. His wrist, he can feel his wrist, the tension in his wrist, he can feel the surging anxiety that someone else will beat him to it. The pulse. But he gets there first. He is first at the other bench, the now vacant bench. And he is first to take the napkin, the green logoed Benjys napkin she used to wipe her tears, and he is first to slip it inside a Di Beradino classic briefcase.

10. The Evian Natural Spring Water 0.75l Nomad bottle

She has the bottle on the reception desk next to her monitor. There is a water cooler. It's not Evian but it is something. Not just tap. But she never has the chance to go to the water cooler. She can't just go to the water cooler whenever she wants. That's not the way it works. Not to say she's chained to the reception. Far from it. She has relief. There's Rita and Emma and Moni. And others. Kelly from marketing but you can't always rely on her. Other girls are more than happy to cover for her. Even though they are obliged to, it's part of their job, they always do it happily, cheerily, they are cheery souls, and if they can't do it they are always ever so sorry. Even Kelly is always ever so sorry. But she can't just up and leave whenever the fancy takes her. It has to be arranged. Even if she wants a toilet break, she has to arrange for someone to cover. The desk can never be left empty.

She doesn't drink tea or coffee, just water. Evian Natural Spring.

Perfect bottled purity

She's thinking of her skin. And she likes the shape of the Nomad bottle. The chubbiness of it. She likes the cleverness of the cap. The blue plastic ring of it. It's comforting to know that there are people somewhere, in France or somewhere, thinking of things that can make her life more convenient, things like the blue plastic ring in the blue plastic cap of the Nomad bottle. You can fix it to your belt, or a strap on your backpack, your rucksack even. It is for backpackers as they take on the world. The new nomads. She imagines herself as a young backpacker with an Evian Nomad fastened to her backpack. She imagines she can feel it bouncing on her backpack as she walks. She imagines herself in Prague, or Rome, or Nice, or Athens, or Budapest, or Dortmund, or one of the other places she sees advertised in the orange Easyjet posters. She imagines herself in khaki shorts, a heavy backpack on her back, slightly sweaty, crammed into a busy metro train in some foreign city at the height of a foreign summer. Alone but happy. She has a map of the city in one of the pockets of her rucksack.

She doesn't have to go there. It is enough that she can imagine herself there. Enough too that she has the Nomad bottle. It does not matter that she has never once used the blue plastic ring for the purpose for which it is designed. It is the possibility of the ring that is important.

You have to be careful what you put into your body. She said that once to some of the young ones, when she was out with some of the young ones, a girls' night out, and of course they laughed, as she knew they would, and of course their laughter was raucous and fierce. The fierce abandon of their laughter perhaps took her aback, perhaps shocked her, but she knew what she was saying when she said it. She is not entirely a fool. Not so naïve as they would believe. There have been men. There was no need for their laughter to be so fierce. It is not so funny that she should say such a thing.

She could fill up the bottle from the water cooler. But she chooses not to. She chooses instead to call into the newsagent's next door, every morning on the way into work, to take a bottle from the refrigerated cabinet, to feel the coldness of the bottle, to grapple with its chubbiness, to hook her finger into the blue plastic ring, to take it to the Indian woman behind the counter, whose name she does not know, but whose smile is familiar and essential, an essential part of her day, whose existence is essential to her, not simply as the vendor of chilled bottled water, but because of the roots. It doesn't matter where you put down roots, you see, as long as you put down roots. Every day of her working life she has exchanged a smile, perhaps a word or two of bland greeting, a word about the weather maybe, with the person sitting behind the counter of the newsagent's. It has not always been the same woman, the Indian woman. It is an office, the office of Donna's water seller. Something akin to the Pope. The Indian woman is simply the latest functionary to perform that office. A smile, a word, a knowing nod – it can never go beyond that. She can never ask the Indian woman her name, nor offer her own. And it is not race, the fact that the woman is Indian, with bindi-smudged forehead, nor class, she has no idea what class or caste even the woman is, or language, the Indian woman speaks perfect English. It is none of these things. The barrier between them is one of function. She feels that the Indian woman understands this and wants it this way too.

evian water is as unique as its origin; 15 years of filtration through the heart of the French Alps

She sips from the bottle now, hastily as she senses that the revolving door is about to revolve and she cannot be caught sipping from the bottle, just as she cannot be caught looking into the mirror of her compact. She sips quickly and places the bottle down next to the monitor, and feels the soft bouncing backlash of the action plastic in her wrist.

It is a group of four. Two of them she recognises. The woman with trendy glasses. She is not a pretty woman but she dresses as though she is. And behaves as though she is. And a tanned man with styled hair. She has seen him before and every time she sees him he looks as though he has come straight from the hairdressers'. He must use product. Or his hair is permed, like his smile appears to be. But that tan. Does he not know that tanning dries out your skin? She'd like to introduce him to her mother, then perhaps he'd take it easy on the sunbed. She knows these two. They are here to see Tony Dawson. She knows that much. These two always ask for Tony Dawson.

She doesn't think she has seen the other two before. She thinks she would remember if she had. One is dressed like a teenage boy, or a rapper, or something: a baseball cap, baggy cut-offs and is that a Hawaiian shirt? But he's somewhere in his thirties, maybe even forties, does he know what he looks like? What does he look like? The other is a fat man with a completely bald head. He stands like he does not believe he is fat, or care. He has a royal blue linen suit on. And sunglasses. Police sunglasses pushed back over his shiny head. He stands like he is an athlete, or famous, a movie actor, everyone says movie nowadays, like he is fit and sexy and famous. But he is a fat man with a bald head that's beginning to glisten. His neck sits in folds.

The guy with the tan carries a large portfolio. They are from the agency. Which is to say BHBY, the advertising agency.

11. The Jammy Dodger

It's because she's a woman. She knows this. And it pisses her off, frankly. But what are you going to do? None of the others would be expected to do it. Not Geoff, not Ian. Not Tony, of course. She wonders if the new one will be the same. Apparently he didn't go down the pub at lunchtime. Maybe he's different.

It's down to her to check the room is set up OK. The biscuits and the thermos jugs with coffee and hot water. Teabags on a plate. Bottles of water, two sparkling, two still. Though why bother with the sparkling these days? These days everyone chooses still.

Do you have everything you need? The easel rattles as she sets it down. She gets a strange look from the fat one. Does he really think he's in with a chance?

There are Jammy Dodgers, she notices. She helps herself to one. Call it a perk. Call it compensation. Call it anger.

She fingertip-rolls a crumb into her mouth. The fat one's watching her, almost licking his lips. Does he want the biscuit or her? she wonders. She smiles to him as she munches on the dual textured mouthful, crunchy biscuit, glutinous jam. The sweetness is intoxicating.

Gooey stretchy jam SPLODGED between two shortbread biscuits.

It is a taste that takes her back, of course. To the gasfire glow of Nan's cosy sitting room. There are always biscuits at Nan's. She can have what she wants at Nan's. Nan dozes as she reads in front of the fire. Her head tips back and the snores start. It is a sweet hot boredom at Nan's. She is bored but she wouldn't wish to be anywhere else. The days last forever at Nan's. The heat is dry. It stretches the surface of her eyes. She feels it in her eyes. And she will doze herself. Her teeth sugar-coated from the biscuits. She can eat as many biscuits as she likes at Nan's. She can eat biscuits and bread and cakes and jam. Whatever she likes. She is never hungry at Nan's. Her teeth fizz at Nan's.

Once she heard Nan fart in her sleep. It was not funny. She did not laugh. It is a secret she guards. She loves her Nan so much. To talk of such a thing, to remember it even, would be a betrayal. But she cannot help remembering, not with the taste of the Jammy Dodger in her mouth.

Even now she guards the secret. Even now that Nan is dead. Even now, ten years after Nan's death, she is loyal to that love.

She wishes she hadn't eaten the biscuit, not with Gina from the agency watching. Not with the fat one watching. Not with all of them from the agency watching.

They wanted to get in the room early.

Sandra swallows. She notices something in the fat one's smirk, as if he's imagining something. Fuck off, she thinks.

Do you need a pad or anything? We have those pads. Or pens?

I've brought my own, says Gina from the agency. And her voice is as crisp and deliberate as her clothes. As bright as her glasses. She smiles.

Haven't seen those for years, he says at last, the fat one.

She affects vagueness. Will not meet his eager eye.

Jammy Dodgers, he explains.

She is regretting that she took the biscuit.

I'm Dave, he says.

Sandra, she answers. He's holding out a hand for her to shake. It is unexpectedly dry.

Perhaps he's only smiling because he's thinking of his own childhood. She can imagine him as a chubby unloved little boy, having been herself a chubby unloved little girl. Except for Nan. Except for the long hot days at Nan's, baking in the overfed heat of Nan's love.

And she is no longer chubby. She has worked hard to shed the puppy fat. Worked herself into hardness.

Where is everyone? says Gina from the agency. Is she nervous? It doesn't seem possible, not with those glasses. But she is helping herself to a glass of water as if she is afraid of drying up.

They hear voices in the corridor and now the others are in the room, Tony, Geoff, Ian and he must be the new one and she is amazed to find that it is him, the guy she saw in Prêt à Manger while she was choosing her Pesto Pasta Salad Bowl. And yet it does not seem so amazing, it seems in fact to be expected, and even she expected it, she finds. For as soon as she saw him she knew that there was or would be something connecting them, something between them. That he would be something to her.

She watches Tony darling-kiss Gina from the agency and wonders has he, has she, have they? She thinks she might be jealous in some obscure unpleasant way and thinks she might even fuck the fat one to get over it. And the new guy's being introduced and he seems scared shitless or something. He's shaking hands with them all and she can see from his face that he's terrified. It's as if he's offering his hand to be mangled by the turning grind of heavy machinery, when all he's doing is shaking hands with the agency. She wants to tell him that it will be all right. She wants to call him Love. Nan always used to call her Love. She wants to see him eat a Jammy Dodger and smile. She wants to know that the sweet sticky crumbling mouthful is taking him back to a time before this troubled time. She can see from his face that he is troubled.

He does not acknowledge that he has seen her before. He does not acknowledge all that passed between them in the Prêt à Manger.

12. The Nobo Brainstormer Flipchart Pad

She hates the way they do this. Keep her waiting. There is Morello, of course, it's to be expected of Morello. They cannot start without Morello. But the rabble from the DM agency? What's their game? And that designer-halfwit.

Tossers, all of them.

It makes her feel better to form the word, tossers, in her mind. It makes it easier to hold the smile across the void.

She likes to play with image. She likes to project the image, crisp professionalism, clipped vowels, she likes to play with the idea of her femininity. The smile. The smile is something you have to see. She knows how to smile and how to communicate nuance through the smile. Her smile is not like Mike's: permanent, unthinking. Her smile is fluid, flexible and alive. She knows the power of withholding it. There is a living tension in her smile. It is a thrilling smile because it seems so precarious. It is a smile that is always on the verge of becoming a pout. The smile is central to the idea of her femininity. The smile is how she does it.

It can be flirtatious, often is. It can be demure. You might even say ladylike. She would not object if you labelled it ladylike. She plays with the idea of being ladylike. It can be coquettish. Then just when she's got you thinking that's how she is, that's what she is, she'll reset the smile, some minute readjustment on the gauge of nuance, and she'll throw out a word, tossers, maybe, or dickhead, dickhead is another of her favourites. And you're still looking at the smile and taking in the crisp professionalism of the clothes, the conscious consummate femininity, what is that scent, you're thinking, and you're reeling. Let's face it, you're shocked. That, at any rate, is the effect she's going for.

The DM rabble and the designer-halfwit come in together in a vague prearranged way that unnerves her. They're all smiles and apologies, Sorry! Sorry! Are you waiting for us? Are we late? Sorry! The traffic across town. You wouldn't believe it. Sorry!

Bollocks. They've been sitting in Coffee Republic over the road, plotting. She has done it enough times herself to recognise the signs.

Bollocks, is another.

Gina holds the smile. Dave and Si are whispering to each other. They are getting bored, she can tell. They have to start this thing soon.

But there is still Morello to wait for. They cannot start without Morello.

She has the marker pen in her hand. She has chosen green. Green is good. The virgin Nobo Brainstormer Flipchart Pad is ready on the easel.

Nobo Brainstormer Flipchart Pad A1 - 40 pages. Thicker top quality paper, specially coated to prevent pens bleeding through to the next page.

Perforated for easy tear-off.

There is a glistening expectancy to its virgin surface. The paper is lit by overhead halogen spots. There is a window, but the light from outside is weak. This is a room at the arse-end of the building, overlooking a sunless alley, the kind of alley drunks stumble into to relieve themselves, if they can be bothered, or couples impatient for sex. You cannot hope for much in the way of light from the window. But that doesn't matter. It is the overhead halogen spots they are here for, the way they pick out the fibrous weave of the paper, and the fine, faint layer of chemical coating, the cream tinge of bleed-proofing.

But then Morello's in the room, filling the room with his easy presence, his relaxed American, is it Californian, she thinks it is, it must be, with his relaxed Californian manner. His slack, effortless charm. He is a good-looking man and he is American and he has what you would call charisma. Even if you had never known charisma in your life, you would recognise it when you met this man. And you would have to admit that you understood why he is one of nature's C.E.O.s.

He can walk into any room late, he can smile his slack easy smile, he can flash his relaxed eyes around the room, any room, maybe even wink, not necessarily at the women, it doesn't have to be at a woman, at anyone he chooses. He can wink at a man. And he can make you forget your anger and he can make you forget that you were waiting for him. You're just glad that he's come at all, glad for his presence filling the room, grateful for him overlapping your existence if only for a moment.

He can do this.

I see new people, he says. Maybe we should do introductions.

She admires the briskness of his entrance, the no nonsense commanding way he dominates the meeting straight from the off, it is never in doubt, he does not do doubt, she admires the confidence, some would call it arrogance, but it is not. Leadership. Leadership is what it is, natural leadership, you cannot teach it.

She's itching to start on the Nobo Flipchart Meeting Pad. She loves the low tack strips on the reverse of the big A1 sheets as much as she loves any part of her job. She loves the crackling excitement of ripping the sheets from the pad.

Perforated for easy tear-off.

And the flapping thrill of tacking them to the wall, any wall. Covering the wall with ideas. Nothing can beat that. She loves the smell of the marker pens. She loves the special coating of the sheets, the eggshell sheen.

Even so, she is willing to postpone all this because of him, because of his charm, his smile, his loping stride as he takes the only place left. She is willing to sit through introductions.

She starts. To get things rolling. She is a great one for getting things rolling. She even says, Shall I start? To get things rolling.

Minimal nods around the room transmit consent.

I'm Gina Andrews, Head of Planning at BHBY.

And so it goes around the room. Name, title, company. Funny how the sense of being the momentary centre transforms each of them in a different way, how they each feel the need to differentiate themselves, to mark their holding of the moment and its passing. It is not a conscious thing, this marking of the moment. It's done with a quick blush, a proto-blush, or the twirl of a pencil, or a flick of the hair, a flick of the head to show off the hair, that's Mike, he is so in love with his hair, or it's done with a shift of the chair, underlined with a scrape, Dave Simmons, Copywriter, BHBY, *screech*. Or it's done with a smirk, or a grimace, or a straightening, or a shiver almost, a spasm almost, Sandra Kirkham, Marketing Manager Diamond Life, or it's done with the click of a biro, or the riffle of a pad, or the whole body tilting forwards. But it's always marked in some way. They cannot let it go with just name, title, company.

And then it gets to the one she's never seen before, the new one. It gets to him and he will not let it go with just name, title, company, she knows. There is something else he wants to say, she knows. Something he has to communicate, something he has to share with the room, she feels this.

I'm Rob Saunders, marketing manager for Diamond Life. I started with the company today…

And that's more than any of them have said, but she knows he will not leave it at that, she can tell he has more to say.

I'm the new boy. The new kid on the block.

There is tension, anxiety around the room. The room cringes. This is not supposed to happen. Name, title, company. Does he not know what is expected of him? Where will this end? None of them knows where this will end.

Finding my feet. Finding my way around.

He's rambling. Somebody put him out of his misery. She should do it but she finds she can't. The words do not come. She finds she has to let him go on.

This morning…

There's a dangerous pause. The pauses are more dangerous than the words with this one. How long will he hold this pause? Someone put him out of his misery. Puh-lease.

I spent some time in Inbound Calls, which was interesting. It's important to spend some time in the different departments, I think, to get a feel for operations. I think that's important. That's what I'd like to do. And this morning…

Again the pause. Why does he insist on pausing there? This morning. Why can he never get past, This morning?

I…

His eyes are scanning the room. What is that she can see in his eyes? Is he going to cry? It looks as if he's going to cry. Somebody put him out of his misery. There is no need for this speech. Does he not know he is not expected to make a speech? Where did he get the idea he was supposed to make a speech?

And no one can say anything because they are waiting to hear what he will say. Finally it comes.

…I had the commute from hell.

In their relief, the communal relief, that he has said something that could plausibly be construed as a joke, they greet the remark with more laughter than it warrants, they drown it in laughter. The guy, the new guy, looks gutted. He looks desperate and frightened and, there's no other word for it, gutted. And she knows that it was not meant as a joke, that there is more he would say if they let him, and she knows that they must not let him.

Morello must have had the same thought, for he is speaking now. He knows it's time to put a stop to this nonsense. And he finds a way to do it that rescues the poor bastard. That saves his stricken face. He makes his own little speech.

I'm Al Morello. C.E.O. of Diamond Life. Yes, I'm American. I too have just joined the company. Been here a little longer than Rob. About a month now, I think it is. Feels like a lifetime.

There's more laughter from around the table. The laughter this time has a different quality. It's not relief. It is knowing. They know what he is doing. They are laughing at his cleverness, at their own cleverness, they are celebrating cleverness. Oh, the cleverness of me, she thinks. And they are laughing at the poor bastard, because he doesn't understand. He has no idea what has happened. How Morello has turned it round, with what charm, ease, good-humour. How Morello has rescued him, rescued them all. How he has made them a gift of his confidence, how he has won them over and relaxed them with calculated candour. How they know all this and appreciate it and celebrate it with modest laughter. Oh, the cleverness of us all. Leaving aside the poor bastard.

I'm usually at my desk by eight a.m.. I find the commute is actually quite pleasant at that time.

And now at last it comes, the Morello wink. And it is genius, it is masterful, for the one he chooses to bestow his wink upon is the poor blurting bastard new guy.

She has the pen in her hand, the cap off the pen, the spirited whiff hits her, assaults her sinuses, but she wants more, she wants to inhale the fume, she wants to breathe deep of the fume. She's standing by the easel with the pen in her hand, the big green marker pen, and the smell is hers alone.

Before you start, Gina, this from Tony, the mess in the suit. Must she put the cap back on the pen? Must she cap the sinus-piercing pang? She gives him a tensing of her smile. Sweetly, sweetly, ever so sweetly, she is saying, How fucking dare you? He does not pick up on it. I just wanted to make sure everyone knows why we're here, he says, not picking up on the subtle modification of her smile.

But no, it's not really about that, is it? It's about you not being able to sit there and let someone else, a woman, let's face it, let's be specific here, let's not beat around the bush, a woman, it's about that, isn't it? That's what this is about. It's about you putting your dick on the table. That's what this is really all about.

Now is a good moment to withhold the smile. You shall not have my smile. Not while you sit there with your dick on the table.

So she downturns the mouth, she quivers the lip, she is not afraid to quiver the lip. When it comes to the quivering of the lip, she has no shame.

Tony, she says. And her voice is crisp and clear. The quiver does not sound in her voice. But recrimination does. Tony, Tony, Tony. She risks touching her forehead with the back of her wrist. She's going for comic effect. She's going for comic wounded. Comic dramatic wounded. She risks, You bastard. And of course they laugh. They realise she's joking, she must be joking. But don't overdo it. Move on quickly. Don't let it become weird. As I was going to say… And the smile bubbles. And the laughter thickens. The reason we're here today. She feels the smile sharpen. The laughter's thinner, but it's still there. They are still with her. Is to look at the brand. To see if we can come to some understanding of what the brand is, what it could be, what it should be. As well as what it isn't. We're here really, Tony darling, to deconstruct the brand. There are no limits. Nothing is taboo. We are amongst friends. We can say whatever we like. Everything gets written down. Nothing gets judged. Or censored. Or censured. If I may indulge in a little parlance, we are here for blue sky thinking. Am I right?

Tony the mess in the suit gives a little side-to-side sashay of the head, which is to say, she is right and she is not right. The blue sky worries me, he confesses. I think we have to keep it real, he insists. We have to be pragmatic.

There is a time and a place for pragmatism, Tony. It is Morello muscling in. On her behalf and she is content to allow him. I want us to think the unthinkable. Let's imagine Diamond Life as we know it does not exist. If it did not exist, what would be in its place? If the brand could be anything we want it to be.

But it can't. The mess in the suit holds his ground. Is he mad? It can't be anything we want it to be.

It turns out Morello is not argument-averse. He counters, But it can. Here, now, in this room. This afternoon.

Fine, concedes Tony. Though I don't really understand what we hope to achieve. What's the point?

The point is to explore. The point is to see what comes up.

And she is standing back waiting for them to finish crossing swords, or dicks, or whatever it is they're crossing. She doesn't have to do a thing. Morello's doing all the work for her.

She gets a nod from him. The Tony guy is sulking in his suit. He's sending little sideways glancing messages to his team, the lesser marketing mortals. She even thinks she catches him rolling his eyes. He should watch it. He should seriously watch it.

I thought we would begin, she begins, by saying what comes to mind when we hear the words Diamond Life. A little bit of word association if you like. So anyone care to begin? Diamond Life? Brings to mind?

This is the bit she loves. The pen hovering over the special coated bleed-proof surface.

Clarity, says Tony. And he gets approving nods from his team, from most of them, the hard-faced Sandra woman, the fat Geoff, the bad-complexion Ian. Only the poor bewildered bastard hasn't the sense to nod.

Her pen squeaks green onto the paper, a sprawl of green. She never bothers to keep the writing legible. Part of the fun is working out what she has written afterwards.

Hardness. This is from Si. You can always count on Si. He tilts his baseball cap down protectively. Or is it defiance?

Value, counters one of the lesser marketing mortals, Geoff, the fat one.

She's writing fast to keep up.

Sharpness. Cutting. Si is not to be intimidated. Comes back with two. It's like some game of poker but it's Si against the lot of them.

Treasure. Fat Geoff again. Jesus. These people.

Elite. It's like some kind of duel.

OK. Elite, did you say? She's playing catch-up with her writing.

Yeah. Elite.

She nods.

The marketing mortals seem intimidated. But Si is determined. He is twisting the knife, the verbal knife. Old fashioned.

That's too much for Tony mess in a suit. Why is a diamond old-fashioned? I don't see that a diamond is old-fashioned. Timeless, yeah. It has a timeless enduring quality.

OK. Timeless. Enduring. These words make it onto the Nobo Brainstormer Flipchart Pad. Her line is slipping. Dropping. The words are getting bigger, too big. She's filled the first page. She rips it off, Hold on, she says as she rips it off. The paper crackles, just as she imagined it would. The huge sheet is unwieldy in her hands. She pats it to the wall, lets the low tack strip on the reverse do its work. They pause to study the words.

I see what you're trying to do here, says Tony, his head trembling. The name is not up for negotiation.

Tony, this is a brainstorm. Everything is up for negotiation. Morello's cool, suavely smiling.

But Al… with all due respect, that name has a heritage in this country. The Diamond symbol has been around for a hundred years. People know what Diamond Life stands for.

And they don't like it, puts in Si. They want something more contemporary.

That's rather a simplistic analysis of market conditions at the moment, if I may say so. The whole financial sector is suffering. The Tony mess is bristling.

We all know that we're trading in adverse conditions, smoothes Morello. We also know that our market share is in free fall. We can't do anything about the former. But we have to address the latter. We have to ask some big questions here. Like what is it we actually do? Can we talk about that for a moment, Gina?

Yeah, sure.

Gina draws a line. It has a little wobble at the end, but other than that, it's a good line.

Underneath the line she writes: WHAT DO WE DO? Some things have to be written in caps.

Anyone care to start? It's a things she says too much, she knows.

Financial services. It's from spotty Ian, one of the lesser marketing mortals, a very lesser one. But even he has the decency to acknowledge his embarrassment with a complicated bit of body language, a shrug is part of it, but also a kind of shrinking, an invisibility craving ripple, a physical summoning of the floor to open up. Gina writes Financial Sercives on the pad. They shout at her she's spelled it wrong. Sercives, sercives, they shout. And she hasn't the foggiest, or pretends she hasn't the foggiest, is she pretending? Then sees her mistake and overwrites the transposition of letters. Look at it, look at it, look at your imaginative barrenness, the desert of your imagination, look how shit you people are, she's saying by drawing their attention to this particular contribution in this way, if this is the best you can come up with, she's saying. This is what we have to deal with, she's saying.

The hard-faced Sandra bitch tries to raise their game. Protection. Peace of mind.

Gina writes these up too. She even says, Lovely, lovely. The idea is not to prejudge, not to censure, not to censor. Not to say, Empty clichés, bitch.

Then the gutted new one, who has been sitting there in a state of bewilderment, as if the whole thing has been conducted in a language foreign to him, the strange gutted new one pipes up.

Life, he says.

There's a swivel of heads towards him. He's the centre of things now. They're all looking at him, waiting for him to explain. They have not demanded an explanation from anyone else but they want an explanation now. Even Gina hesitates before touching the green spewing tip to the bleed proof surface.

I mean, it's all about life, isn't it. I don't mean just life assurance. I mean, we're there for them throughout their life. Even if it's just… making sure the roof gets repaired. It's their life. And they turn to us. And then there are the big life moments. The first home. Saving for a wedding. The birth of a child. We want them to turn to us. We want them to see us as part of their life. Part of those moments. If they invest in us, they're investing in life.

The heads swivel towards Morello, awaiting his reaction. It is a poised moment. The poor gutted bastard's fate is poised. Morello is like the Roman emperor at the games. The poor gutted bastard is the gladiator awaiting the thumb, the life or death thumb. Morello seems to nod, minutely. His reaction is contained, but it just might be favourable.

There is a collective relaxing. Gina touches the green-leeching bullet point onto the Nobo Brainstormer Flipchart Pad, A1.

OK, life, she says as she writes. Life, she writes.

13. **The Ideal-Standard Space btw wc**

He's hugging the bowl, the seat is up, the cover and the seat are up, he's down on his knees, hugging the bowl, studying the writing, the logo, Ideal-Standard, hugging the vitreous china bowl, breathing the toilet smell, inhaling the cold clammy comfort. But the toilet doesn't do it. The toilet doesn't do it for him. The Di Beradino is under his desk. The Di Beradino with the Snoopy ring binder and the Benjys napkin. Only the Di Beradino classic with its emotion-heavy freight, one death-charged, one tear-stained, only that can comfort now.

Highly space efficient back-to-wall WC suite with washdown bowl and box flushing rim. Space WC pans have design matched seats and covers which can be fitted so as to make best use of the area available.

- *Highly space efficient*
- *Choice of seat configuration*
- *Part of space efficient*

He wants to be sick. He feels it is expected of him. He came in here not feeling sick. Not the slightest taste of nausea, not the first belch-pressure of a heave, the needle-trip shifts intimating purgation, barely registered. He came in here feeling the need to do something, to give something back. Feeling the need to go somewhere and make an offering. He thought the toilet smell would do it. He thought perhaps he'd hug the bowl, maybe get his nose up close to some dubious stains, some yellow congealing round the rim, some deep dark skid marks. He had the feeling if he did, that would do it. But the toilet is spotless. So he's relying on the smell of disinfectant, the leech of blue from the plastic cage hooked under the rim. But it's not working. He can give nothing. Nothing comes. Not even tears.

He wants to get this over and done with, so he can get back to his desk and check up on the Di Beradino and its contents. It scares him to think that someone might have stolen the case. Things go missing. He's left it unattended. It would be an easy thing to do. He must get back to his desk, back to the briefcase. He makes a promise to the case, or to the gods, God, to whoever handles these things, he makes a promise that he will never leave it unattended again.

So it's the finger in the throat, he has to resort to the finger down the throat. He closes his eyes on tears now, that's good, that's good, the tears have come. Physiology is taking over. You cannot fight the finger. The convulsion shocks. The loss of control is total. He was not expecting it to be so quick, so complete, so devastating. But this is what he needs. He needs to become this. Out of control. A body in reverse. The All Day Breakfast heaving up, back up, there dry and big and difficult and hurting in his throat, finger hand out of the way now. And it's like coming, a big ugly dirty kind of coming.

He's dizzy and empty. He cannot stand. He cannot tear himself away from the bowl. But he must get back to the Di Beradino.

14. **The Hugo Woman fragrance**

She likes the smell. That is the first thing to be said. She would not use it if she did not like the smell. For instance, Jean Paul Gaultier Classique. She likes the bottle. Loves that bottle. She is one of the ones who loves that crazy bottle. But she does not like the smell, the scent if you like, but she prefers to say smell. She just doesn't like it. And she likes the ads for Calvin Klein, for CK Be, the Kate Moss ads remember. She likes those ads and she likes Kate Moss, but she's not mad about the smell. It's OK, but she prefers Hugo Woman. Perhaps it's something to do with the fact that CK Be is unisex. She doesn't quite get that unisex thing. She's honest enough to know that it might be about something other than the smell, something else as well as the smell. But the smell is important. She has to like the smell. Otherwise, no. She wouldn't use it if she didn't like the smell, if there wasn't something about the smell that she likes, that does it for her, that comforts. She loves the run up to Christmas, those ads you see in the run up to Christmas, the commercial breaks crammed full of perfume ads, crazy ads, the crazy Obsession ads. Obsession too. She likes the Obsession ads. She wishes she worked for a perfume manufacturer, she'd love to be marketing perfume, maybe one day, but now, today, here, it's something else. It's very far from perfume. She knows that she will never work for a parfumier. She knows it is too late for that. She should have thought about that earlier. Her experience is financial. You do not generally make the leap from financial to perfume. She has never heard of anyone yet making that leap. Besides, you have to build on what you have. A leap would be something new. A leap would be a step back in some respects. Financially, she is thinking. As far as her own financial package is concerned.

The smell, or scent if you'd rather, goes with her. She has just freshened up. A dab on the wrist. Another on the neck. Dab the wrist to the neck. Not much. You don't need much. She is coming out of the Ladies' room, fresh and fragrant, Hugo woman surrounded by Hugo Woman.

Hugo woman is independent of mind and means. She's smart, confident and she doesn't need permission – she does what she wants. No limits, no compromise. She's an original – her fragrance is Hugo Woman.

The thing is you have to make a choice. You have to decide on one. You have to have the confidence to make a choice. You cannot be overwhelmed. You have to be clear in your mind. Confidence comes from clarity. Choice comes from confidence. And she has made her choice. Hugo Woman.

As she comes out she sees him, Rob what-was-his-name. Rob Something. The new one. She sees him. He's slumped against the wall. His head is thrown back. His face is very pale. His eyes are closed. Perhaps she can get past without his seeing her. Repay him for the way he blanked her earlier. Get him back for Prêt à Manger.

As she forms the thought, he opens his eyes and they go straight to hers. Again Sandra feels there is something between them.

You all right? she says.

He nods.

That's all right then, she thinks but does not say. She does not smile. She knows she is not a great one for smiling. She does not find it easy or natural for some reason, which is not to say she is miserable, she feels she is quite happy thank you very much, but she does not see the need to smile. Besides, there is nothing she hates more than the false smile. She is thinking of Gina from the agency. Jesus, can that girl smile. But she doesn't envy her her smile because she knows it is false. It is plastic and false and she hates it.

Apparently the Russians are like this, naturally unsmiling. She has read that. Perhaps she has Russian blood in her. She doesn't even smile at the thought, though it amuses her.

The thing is, he is all right. He nodded in response to the question, so he is all right. That's fine then. She can get on. She can walk past him, leave him. There is nothing between them, whatever she feels. She is naturally suspicious of her feelings.

The last thing she should do is trust her feelings. And it's not as if she doesn't have things to do.

So she walks past him, she gets a good five paces past him, then she stops. The image of his pale, stricken face will not go away. She turns around. She walks back to him. She stands in front of him, close to him. She looks into his eyes. His eyes have many colours in them. There is green and amber and russet, if russet is a colour, she thinks it is, his eyes, his irises, are like little apples, she realises.

You're not all right, are you?

I've had the weirdest day. You wouldn't believe it.

What?

Well. This morning. He shakes his head. No, it's all right. There's no reason to…

Tell me.

I saw a girl throw herself in front of a tube train.

Shit. You poor thing.

She puts a hand on his cheek. She does not think or question. It just goes there.

She doesn't need permission

I just puked up. Delayed reaction, I suppose.

Sandra keeps her hand there.

That's all right.

She keeps looking at his little apple eyes.

I have a girlfriend. We live together.

That's all right too.

Sandra smiles. Remember, she is not a natural smiler, does not find it easy to smile. Then, finally, she takes her hand away.

Look after yourself, she says.

She walks on, without looking back. She feels him watching her go. Rob Saunders, she remembers. She feels him tilt his head gently back against the wall and close his eyes. She feels him breathe Hugo Woman, the few potent molecules she has scattered for his comfort.

15. The Mulholland Brothers Messenger Bag

The bag, of course, it is not a briefcase if you don't mind, the bag is a Mulholland Brothers Messenger Bag. They're standing on the steps outside, they have just come through the revolving door, the new guy squeezing himself into the same section of the revolving door, he's seriously wondering about the new guy, there's something seriously odd about this guy, squeezing up next to him like that, is he gay, he wonders. They pop apart as the swinging door expels them, caught in the momentum of the swing. They eye each other's bags, and he has to admit the other guy's is nice, a nice bag, nice choice, it reassures him, that he might have made the right choice, that he may not be such a chump as he seems. And he's waiting for Rob to ask him about his own bag, his Mulholland Brothers Messenger Bag because he's dying to tell him the story. Because, although Rob's bag is nice, it cannot compare with the Mulholland Brothers Messenger Bag. Does not come close. No bag can.

He's preparing the story in his head, I bought it in the States, he's forming. He's experimenting, mentally, with a casual throw-away delivery. Maybe he'll drop the I. Bought it in the States. That's all it needs.

Tony feels sure a question's coming. The new boy cannot take his eyes off that bag.

In Los Angeles, he'll add. Beverley Hills. Maybe he should start with Beverley Hills? Bought it in Beverley Hills. Maybe that's all it needs?

But the question doesn't come. Maybe he should start the ball rolling by complimenting Rob on his bag? Put the idea in his head to do the same, and on the reciprocation, hit him with the story.

Mulholland Brothers Messenger Bag. The bag was made famous by the Pony Express riders who helped build the West.
Features: Padded adjustable shoulder straps.
Padded top carry handle.
Exterior pocket with snap-buckle closure.

Interior adjustable strap top closure with adjustable pull tab. Interior divider.

That was some trip. That was some time of his life.

But the whole thing's bollocks, of course. And nothing could be naffer than complimenting a guy on his briefcase just because you want him to say something nice about your bag. Tony knows this. He is not unaware of how this makes him appear. So he says nothing about Rob's case, keeps quiet about that. Maybe later. Maybe he will tell the story later. There is always later. Work it in somehow later.

Fancy a quick pint?

Rob's frown is vaguely persecuted but he says, OK. I guess I could do with a drink after all.

You guess? You're starting to sound like Morello.

They're walking now.

I think he liked your little speech.

It takes the guy a second to get on the wavelength. His frown is questioning. Then it dawns. Oh. I was just rambling.

I think you made an impression.

I don't know whether it was a good impression. I think I made a bit of a fool of myself.

Tony does not contradict him.

The Honey-brown Lariat leather contains waxy tannins that surface over time, enhancing the natural marks and scratches of daily use. Lariat leather has a genuine, soulful character that just gets better with time.

You ever been to America? he says. It seems natural coming out of the talk of Morello, the talk of Americanisms. It does not seem forced. At least he hopes it doesn't. But it leaves the door open.

Yes, says Rob.

Whereabouts?

New York, New Orleans, the West Coast.

Tony nods approvingly. Los Angeles?

Yes, I spent some time in Los Angeles.

And Tony wants to bring in the bag but he doesn't know if he can just yet. It seems kind of sudden. So he says instead, What did you think?

And Rob blows out his cheeks, he seems startled by the question, defeated, as if this is the last question he expected, but surely he must have expected it, they were talking about America, after all, and he claims he's been there.

I didn't like it, he says. I didn't like LA.

They carry on in silence. Tony decides he won't tell the new guy about the bag, the story behind the bag. It will be wasted on him, he decides.

16. The pint of London Pride

He doesn't even know what pint to order. That's how shot he is. He's clutching the Di Beradino and getting anxious about what beer to order. Will he make the right choice? They will judge him on his choice. For they are all here, his new colleagues, Ian, Geoff, Sandra, already ensconced, funny how that word is only ever used about people in pubs, or seems only to be, he picks up on these things, being in marketing, a marketing man, a professional. But he is tired of that word, that particular word, ensconced. It is not one of the words he loves.

They are ensconced around a high circular leaning table, presenting their backs to him, or at least the men are and he has no idea what to order.

He looks at the bar for clues, guidance. It is a tiny bar, a tiny pub, and packed. Packed with loud braying suits. He squeezes his hand around the handle of the Di Beradino. Tony will turn to him any moment and say,

What can I get you?

In the end he doesn't have to think about it. The choice has already been made. London Pride, he says. A moment ago, he thought he might be tempted into lager, a Kronenberg or something. Stella. The others, the other men are drinking lager, and he felt that lager was expected of him, that London Pride will be seen as eccentric, will raise a few eyebrows. And he doesn't want that. Not on his first day, not after all that has happened. A moment ago he had no idea he would ask for London Pride. But now he realises that is what he wants. And he wants it in a dimple pot. He is afraid to ask but he hopes that it comes in a dimple pot. He will take it as some kind of sign if it comes in a dimple pot, not a straight glass, a schooner. There will be no comfort in that, he feels.

Maybe it is something in the air. The air is beer-soaked. The air carries memory molecules of London Pride. That's what comes through most. The air made the decision for him.

Anyone else? Tony asks.

But there are no takers. They have only just got in, and nod to their nearly full glasses.

He moves closer to the others. But the men, Ian and Geoff, turn minutely away from him, give him more of their backs than he had before. It is subtle and maybe it doesn't happen at all, or they do not realise they are doing it, maybe they do not realise it. Certainly they do not realise it. He cannot believe they would do it knowingly. But it does not come over as very friendly. Quite the opposite. They're closing him out. That's how it feels. He is not welcome, is how it feels.

It is a crowded pub. Perhaps they are only responding to the pressures of the place.

At any rate, she does not join in. She turns to him. She looks him fully, frankly in the face. She swivels on her high stool, she has managed to nab a stool, you feel she would always be able to secure a stool for herself. He feels her gaze searching his eyes. For something.

She asks, How you feeling now?

So it will be acknowledged. She will acknowledge what passed between them. He must do the same.

Better thanks.

Her head bobs in a little upward nod. She does not smile. She seems stubborn about this not smiling.

Not going home to the girlfriend?

Y-yes. I'm just having a quick pint first.

What's she called?

Julia.

Julia. It's a nice name. I expect she's a nice girl.

She does not smile.

Yes.

What does she do?

She's a teacher.

Teacher. Very worthy.

Infants. The pay isn't great but… she's very good at it.

It's a vocation.

That's what they say.

It must be nice to have one of those.

You don't?

You are joking? A vocation? For this?

How did you… uh, get into this game?

I suppose you could say it was a love of money. I didn't have any of my own so I wanted to be close to other people's. She sips her drink, white wine, large glass. Probably chardonnay, he thinks. She sips it, to mark a turn in her thoughts. A turn back to Julia. You get good pensions in education. I remember that from my FA days.

There is that. Do you have…?

A pension?

It is almost grim the way she doesn't smile.

No. A boyfriend. Why does he want to know this? he wonders.

Better than that.

She holds out her hand and shows Rob a ring. There are depths of colour in the diamonds. He can see purple, blue, green. They are amazingly vibrant colours. He has never really understood the thing about diamonds, about jewellery, until now. Now he thinks he could stare at those diamonds forever.

We've been engaged for two years.

That's… wonderful.

Is it?

I don't know, he confesses. You tell me. Is it?

It doesn't always feel wonderful. I love him to bits, of course. I just wish he would hurry up and make an honest woman of me. She sips from her drink. She's hiding her face in the over-sized wine glass. Then she looks up and locks her gaze onto his. Before I go and do something… dishonest. The effort of holding the look is too much. She starts blinking. She blinks excessively and seems to shiver. The over-blinking is fascinating to watch, but appalling too. Perhaps it is instead of smiling, he thinks. Perhaps she has developed a whole repertoire of facial and bodily tics to compensate for her inability, or unwillingness, to smile.

He feels sorry for her. He wants to do something to make her smile. He wishes she didn't have such a hard face. Yes, it is a face he would describe as hard. He wants to soften it. He wants to find a way to soften it.

He wants to fuck her.

In the end he has to look away. It is the blinking. Too much blinking.

He looks to the bar to see how Tony is getting on. He's anxious about that dimple pot, he realises. But Tony is still waiting to be served, isn't even at the bar. He sees Rob looking and shrugs, glum, resentful.

Rob looks back to her, Sandra, to see how she is getting on with her blinking. It is spent, the fit. He can talk to her now. Find a way to soften her face.

So, he asks, you used to be a financial adviser?

For my sins. How about you?

Geoff and Ian angle themselves to listen to Rob's answer.

No, I haven't ever been a financial adviser.

What have you been?

Well, I started off at P&G. Graduate trainee, you know.

Something you would describe as a snigger comes from one of them. Ian it is. Rob turns to him questioningly, but Ian busies himself drinking his lager.

It's hardly the same, is it? explains the other one, the Geoff one. It is funny, how one of them sniggers and the other one explains. Selling soap powder and selling financial services, explains the Geoff one.

And then I had a spell agency side. My client was HSBC.

There is something grudging in their body language.

So why d'you give up all that and come and work for a fucked-up firm like Diamond Life? She's blinking again. For blinking, read smiling, he has worked out.

I suppose I like a challenge.

Either that, or you must have done something very bad in a former life.

Something like that.

At last Tony is there with the drinks, two dark pints, in dimple pots, the handles clutched in one hand. Tony holds both pints out to Rob and he knows what is expected of him, for once today he knows what is expected of him. He takes the pints, one in each hand, allowing Tony to release his grip. Then he hands one pint back to Tony. They nod to each other. A difficult manoeuvre successfully executed.

What are you having? asks Rob.

London Pride, says Tony lifting the pot to his lips and downing nearly half of it in a succession of big noisy gulps. Rob is elated, it's close to elation, what he feels, at this vindication. These are the things that give us confidence. He made the right choice.

Cheers, says Rob. And he adds, Thanks Tony, because he does not feel, he never does feel, that cheers is enough.

And he sips from his own pint.

London Pride is a smooth and astonishingly complex beer, which has a distinctive malty base complemented by a rich balance of well developed hop flavours from the target, challenger and northdown varieties in the brew. At 4.1% a.b.v in cask (4.7% a.b.v in bottles)London Pride is an ideal session-strength premium ale.

I needed that, says Tony. What a day.

And Rob catches her eye, catches her watching him, looking out for him even, he might even believe she's looking out for him. And if he concentrates on her eyes, looks only at her eyes, ignores what she's doing with her mouth, or the rest of her face, but just concentrates on her eyes, he can see she's smiling, and the smile is worth something, worth everything, because he knows it's for him alone.

17. The Sabatier Au Carbone 8 inch Carbon Steel Chef's Knife

She knows how easy it is to get caught up in your day.

She is in the kitchen, chopping mushrooms. She chops carefully, methodically. She thinks about what she is doing. The knife, she knows, is very sharp. She will not drink until she has finished chopping.

She pictures him with the briefcase. She smiles at the thought of him with the briefcase. The briefcase was a hit. The memory of his face when he saw the case uplifts her.

She looked into it. She researched it. She thought he would like it.

She has a CD playing. She has chosen Gesualdo. She could just as easily have chosen Beck. But tonight it is Gesualdo. The music soothes.

When Rob comes home, they will have a drink. She'll quarter the lime with the knife, the Sabatier. The Sabatier Au Carbone 8 inch Carbon Steel Chef's Knife. It will glide through the pips. She won't even know the pips are there.

They like to live this life. A life of quartered limes and Sabatier knives. Though sometimes she thinks, Who are we trying to kid?

The knife is balanced in her hand. The blade is heavy. The blade is mottled and discoloured. That is the thing with carbon steel. It is not stainless steel. She could have chosen stainless steel but she researched it. She researched it and decided carbon steel is best. She loves the feel of it in her hand. She loves the pull of the weight of the blade. The gravity in it. She loves the way the blade pulls down in her hand, like it's eager to be at the cutting. Like it's hungry for cutting. She loves the restraining snag in the handle. And the rivets. She loves the rivets, she can feel the rivets in the black resin handle, or she knows they are there but she thinks she can feel them. Her knowledge of them is tangible. She went for black resin. There are Sabatiers with wooden handles and others with steel handles. She went for black resin. She went for carbon steel. These knives were her choice, her insistence. She researched it. Part of it was research. Part of it was feeling. The black resin sang to her. The carbon steel sang to her. She knew when she saw them. She knew when she felt them in her hand, the eager pull. They have the set of them. She went into it with her eyes open. The carbon steel. The discolouring. She has had cheaper knives but never been happy with them. Not wholly. Not really. Not happy like she is now with the Sabatiers. She loves the feel of the knife as it cuts through the mushrooms. The knife gets lost in the sucking moistness of the parting mushroom. It is never out of control, but it pulls.

Or Nelly Furtado, she could have chosen Nelly Furtado. But tonight she wants Gesualdo, she wants madrigals, she wants soothing. With all the strangeness of Gesualdo, she finds Gesualdo soothing.

She doesn't blame him for not calling. For not finding a moment to call her. Maybe he had a moment but he knew she would be in class. He could have left a message on her mobile but maybe he didn't want to leave a message. Maybe he wanted to talk to her in person. Maybe there's something wrong with the network. He tried to leave a message but it didn't work. She always wonders about that.

She knew they would require some sharpening. She expected them to be blunt when she got them home. Her research had warned her about that. She knew she would have to get them sharpened.

She doesn't blame him but she worries. She has a tendency to worry.

The mushrooms are chestnut mushrooms. She has wiped them clean with a piece of damp kitchen roll. You do not rinse mushrooms. You wipe them clean. Rob always rinses mushrooms, he leaves them bobbing in a sink of cold water. She tells him not to. She tells him you have to wipe mushrooms. He says it's OK to soak them. She calls him Rob and tells him it's not OK. Rob, she says, Rob. She knows she's doing it, but she can't stop. Talking to him like he's one of her children. A child.

She knows he hates it. Rob, she says, you do not soak mushrooms, you wipe them.

She has that note in her voice. He hates it. She hates it too.

She wants to have heard from him. She wants to know how he has got on on his first day. She wishes he had found the time to let her know when he will be home. She has thought about him. She wonders if he has thought about her at all. She knows he will have been busy. She hopes it went OK. She thinks it strange he has not called.

She trims the stems and puts the discarded ends in the discarded packaging. These are organic mushrooms, prepackaged. She does not approve of the packaging but sometimes it happens. Sometimes you have no choice.

She talks to the children in her class about litter. She tells them about pollution. She feels a hypocrite. She has not told them that sometimes you have no choice.

The knives sit in a wooden knife block. They have the complete set. They go some way towards compensating her for this tiny galley kitchen. You cannot swing a cat but what does it matter if you have a complete set of Sabatier steels.

They require some sharpening in the beginning. She remembers the sharpening now. She remembers taking them to the hardware store on Park Road. She did some ringing round, she is the type of person who rings round. It is important to find someone who knows how to sharpen carbon steel. It is not like stainless steel. Rob thought she was mad. Rob was going to sharpen them himself. Rob thought she was mad buying a set of blunt knives. He was outraged that they had been sold a set of blunt knives. He did not understand about the sharpening. She went into it with her eyes opening about the sharpening. She called round shops, hardware stores, she got the Thomson Local out, the Yellow Pages. She rang them all. It was not a question of price. She was not comparing prices. She was looking for someone who knew what they were doing.

- *Versatile knife for chopping and slicing*
- *Carbon steel blade, full tang and bolster*
- *Riveted polypropylene handle*

- *Hand wash*
- *Made in France*

She was looking for someone to show some knowledge of carbon steel. Of Sabatier. She was looking for a sign that they knew what they were doing. It was the fact that the guy laughed. They guy laughed when she told him she had a set of Sabatier Au Carbones. He laughed with pleasure, with simple delight. Well, you know your knives, he said. And so she went with him.

The bolsters are the shoulders of the blade, the bits that stick out just where the blade goes into the handle. The tang is the part of the blade that extends into the handle. She knows this from her research. She came across the words in her research and, being the sort of person she is, she had to get to the bottom of them. She could not let them go. If she comes across a word she doesn't know the meaning of, maybe a familiar word used in an unfamiliar way, like tang and bolster, words like this, she has to look them up. She cannot stand to let them go. She cannot stand that sense of uncertainty, the sense of missing out, it is a kind of loss she feels, an emptiness. And she is a teacher, so she feels a professional duty to understand the world and its words, the words like tang and bolster that define some part of it.

She would have found time to call, she thinks. She would have left a message.

You cannot put carbon steel knives in the dishwasher. Some Sabatiers are stainless steel. But the professionals prefer carbon. They require some sharpening in the beginning but the thing is they hold their sharpness. Once you have sharpened them, they stay sharp. This is what her research had led her to believe. This is what swung it.

She is familiar with each blotch and blemish on the blade. She has come to cherish the discolouration.

Do you want me to grind down the bolsters so I can sharpen the blade at the back? he asked. She smiles now at the memory of that question, her pleasure in it.

She has not been disappointed in the knives. She loves the way they have held their sharpness.

An excellent knife maker, Sabatier is one of the few companies left that still make a line of pure carbon steel blades--they take a sharp edge better than any other material. For many chefs, this sharp edge more than makes up for minor discolorations that occur with age.

She looks out of the window, between the pale leaves of the London planes, down onto the street. She's looking for him. He has not rung. She's expecting him. She does not know whether to start the cooking. But she's hungry.

She has only four mushrooms left to slice.

She did not get him to grind down the bolsters.

She wonders if she should call Rob. But decides against it. She wants to do something with her worry, call someone. She thinks about calling mum. She will spend a little time worrying about mum. Then she will call her. She thinks maybe she is not being honest. Maybe she didn't think about him at all today. Maybe she didn't find a moment to think about him. Maybe she didn't notice he hadn't called until now, when she's hungry and she wants to know if she should start the dinner.

She's trying to compensate, trying to prove to herself that she cares. He will come home when he comes home. If he doesn't come home soon she will call him. Or maybe she will call mum.

She makes herself think about mum. It makes her feel guilty but she realises she must do this. It makes her feel afraid but she knows there is no way to avoid this.

If she is afraid, how much more afraid will mum be? It is this thought that lies behind her guilt.

She starts on the onions. Wanting the tears.

She feels discordant. She wants tears but she is not tearful, not truly tearful, not honestly so. The music is soothing but she cannot be soothed. Perhaps she chose the wrong CD. She is annoyed, she admits at last. She is annoyed and worried and afraid, she tells herself she is afraid for mum, but it's for herself she's afraid. She's afraid of mum's loneliness and mum's ageing and the processes at work in mum's body, but she knows that they will be the same processes at work in her own body before too long. Soon enough.

That's the thing about being a teacher, the children you teach, even when you do not have children of your own, the children you teach, they are human clocks, as they grow and progress through the school they mark off the years for you.

The thought of her mother makes her lonely.

But she likes the feel of the knife in her hand. There is some compensation in the feel of the knife in her hand. But they do not have the room, they do not have the surfaces, the work surfaces. Even the knives cannot stop her feeling discordant.

She wants to ask him for a new kitchen. She wants to talk about moving, to see what he thinks. She feels a sense of urgency.

18. Sloggi Basic midi briefs

She's chopping the chicken now. She has the mushroom chopped, the onion chopped, the garlic crushed. This is the way she does it. Vegetables first, then she moves on to the chicken. She changes the chopping board but keeps the same knife.

She hates the feel of raw meat in her hand. Handling raw meat she always thinks she ought to be a vegetarian. But when it's cooked it's all right.

It's hard too when they have done animal stories in class. The children don't quite get the connection, between the animals in their stories and the dead meat on their plates, but she does.

She loves the sharpness of the knife. There is nothing worse than a blunt knife on raw meat. You have to really work the knife. There is a danger you will mash the meat, mangle it, at least at the edge. A blunt knife makes you handle the meat for longer. You really have to grip the meat with a blunt knife.

But the knife is sharp, it is a Sabatier au Carbone 8 inch Carbon Steel Chef's knife, and it is a joy, apart from the touching of the meat, the raw meat, apart from that it is a joy to see the knife glide through the chicken. She barely has a sense of the meat's resistance, of the meat's cohesion, of its unwillingness to be cleaved. She barely has a sense of the meat as meat. It seems the meat is complicit in its own slicing. That it welcomes it. It seems the meat parts itself almost you would think before the blade touches it, so instant is its sundering, so as it were preordained. The knife's participation seems merely ritualistic. The blade is the summoner of the slicing, it does not actually slice, you might believe. The touch required being so light, so almost magical. The thing is, it's over quickly when the knife is sharp.

She is quick to wash her hands. She is always quick to wash her hands after handling raw meat. She always lets the water run hot and uses hand wash lotion. She will not have soap in the kitchen. Soap in the kitchen is a breeding ground for germs. They have a bottle of Sainsbury's own brand hand wash by the sink. She likes the fact that it is clear, clear bottle, clear liquid, with just the right viscosity. She likes the bottle. The shape of the bottle is simple but elegant. She likes the writing on the bottle, the design of the letters. They have done something clever with the e and G of extra Gentle. They have turned the e upside down, just flipped it on its horizontal axis, to form a G. To make it work, they have cheated a little on the e. The line of the e is incomplete, which catches the eye in a pleasing way. This is the sort of thing that he draws her attention to. She likes it when he does. She feels included in his world.

Even own brand is a choice.

The pan is on the stove with the oil already in it. A little groundnut oil.

She hears the outside door bang. She hears steps on the stairs. The stairwell there has that gloomy, undecorated feel of all communal stairs. A temporariness. And it is grubby. You have to run at the stairs to get past the despondency, to prevent it pulling at your heart. Otherwise you would never make it into the flat. Usually she can recognise his steps. He always gets up the stairs as quickly as he can. They both do. Usually it is the pounding hurry of his steps that gives him away. But these are not his steps. She does not think these are his steps. They are slow, arrhythmic, halting. They are not the steps of someone who takes the stairs at a run.

She hears the door to the flat. It must be him. The discordance does not go. She expected the discordance to go as soon as he stepped through the door. But she still feels the discordance.

The notes of the Gesualdo come like beautiful sobs. Tristis est mea anima. The sobs wash over her like waves of sadness. The beautiful sadness soaks into her.

What does she expect when she listens to Gesualdo?

Tri-
sti-
ssssss
e-
st
me-
a

An overlapping of sorrow.

He is home. It must be him. But he has said nothing. She would have expected him to call out. To come into the kitchen maybe. To kiss her. To tell her how his day has gone. His first day.

She would have expected a more pronounced happiness. A simpler joy. To be able to discard her loneliness, to move away from her fear. And now she finds she has to work at these things.

She puts a flame under the oil and calls out, Is that you?

Still he does not answer. There is a throb of fear in her quickening pulse. Maybe it isn't him?

Rob?

She adds the crushed garlic and the chopped onion to the pan.

You haven't eaten have you?

She wonders if she imagined the sounds of the doors. Was it wishing him here that she heard?

I'm in the kitchen.

She lifts the other chopping board, the board with the chicken on and holds it over the pan. Then thinks better of it. She puts the board back down in its space on the work surface.

She lowers the flame. Something makes her lower the flame.

He is sitting on the sofa with his head in his hands. He is hiding his face in his hands.

The briefcase she bought him that lit up his face is on the floor at his feet. The angle of his head is towards the briefcase. But he is covering his eyes. She has the thought that he is hiding his face from the briefcase.

She says, Hi? She can feel the air vibrate her flesh, the flesh of her throat as she says, Hi? It is a throb in her throat.

Tri-

sti-

ssssss

He does not lower his hands. He does not lift his head. He does not take his head out of his hands. He does not look at her. He begins to shake. His shoulders begin to shake.

Rob? Rob? What is it?

She goes over to the sofa. She joins him on the sofa.

She pulls at his hands. The hands do not resist. It does not take much to get him to drop the hands after all. She sees tears. She sees a face drenched in tears.

His eyes are closed. His shoulders are no longer shaking. He throws himself back into the sofa. He keeps his eyes closed tight.

What is it? What happened?

Something must have happened.

Rob shakes his head. He keeps his eyes closed, screws them tight, as he shakes his head in fierce denial.

His eyes open. He does not look at her, not directly. But that his eyes are open now is something. He looks around her. He is aware of her presence. He must be, by the way he fastidiously avoids looking at her.

His hands are on her. His hands are pulling at her. He pulls her towards him down on top of him. He pulls at her. He is like a blind man pulling at her. His mouth finds hers. His avid mouth. She cannot remember when he ever kissed her like this. She does not believe he ever has. It is not kissing, it is breathing. She is his vital element. She is his oxygen. She feels this. She worries vaguely about the pan over the heat. She realises that this is more important than the pan. For him. For both of them. She realises that there is nothing more important now than this way he is kissing her, inhaling her by kissing her. It is not pleasant. It is essential. She is essential to him, she realises. He is trying to breathe her in. She is a solid body. It's crazy. You cannot breathe in a solid body. But this is what he is trying to do. It is not pleasant, it is not gentle, it is not proficient. It is crazy. It is moving. She is moved by his need for her, by this crude, blind, angry need. Being so moved she is aroused. His mouth explores her face, latching on, palpating, trying to breathe her in, seeking out the place that will allow this. His hands are pulling at her clothes. He stops kissing her, the desperate crazy breathing kissing stops as he pulls back. She looks at his face. Still he avoids looking at her. She realises he is afraid to look at her and she is moved by this too. Aroused by this. His fear touches her. It inspires her with tenderness. She wants to be so tender and giving for him. She wants to show him, she wants to prove to him. She wants to move him. Out of his fear. She helps him work the top over her head. She thinks about the pan. She imagines the pan in flames. She imagines the kitchen in flames. She wants to go into the kitchen to switch off the heat. But her top is off now and he is trying to breathe her in again. His mouth is seeking out a place on her body that will allow him to inhale her. His hands are at the strap of her bra. His incompetence moves her. She helps him. For her it is a simple thing, a deft, she does not even think of it as deft, a natural reaching behind. She feels the moment of her breasts' exposing. It is a moment of liberation, it is a moment of joy. She throws back her head to celebrate the moment. It is a moment of purpose. She throws back her head because it will make her breasts stand out more. She wants this effect. She wants it for him, for both of them. She wants his palping mouth to start on her breasts, to start inhaling, to start trying to inhale her through her breasts. She feels it now, his mouth and his hands are on her tingling breasts, answering the tingling of her breasts. And now she is working at his tie, and she is always as incompetent with the tie as he is always incompetent with the bra. He helps her, he allows one hand to help her with the tie. That is all he allows to be diverted from the act of trying to breathe her in. She gets the tie off, with his help. His hand goes back to her breast. She must get on with unbuttoning his shirt without its help. She thinks about the pan. She unbuttons his shirt. She thinks about the pan. The flame is low. The labour of the unbuttoning. She is sure she set the flame low. Let the onions burn. Let them blacken. It is the catching fire she worries about. She worries about burning down the flat. Burning down the house. Burning down the street. The smell of the onions reminds her of her hunger. The onions will be cooked by the time they have finished. The house will not burn down. She is prepared for the onions to be burnt. She is preparing herself for this. But the pan will not catch fire. The labouring of the unbuttoning is over. His shirt is undone. She reaches a hand towards the short sparse hairs of his chest. It is wistful, almost, this reaching. But he is pushing her back and she gives in to his pushing, for she understands its purpose. He pushes her back, her giving in to the pushing, until she is lying on her back on the sofa. He is at the fastening of her trousers, his hands are there. He is pulling down her trousers. And she is helping him. She is keeping her legs together to help him. He unsheathes her legs. His mouth is breathing her in again, trying to find a place on her legs, naked now, through which he can inhale her. His mouth gapes and latches on to the sense-zones of her legs. Each zone has a different sensitivity. Each zone responds differently to the gentle sucking action of his mouth, so gentle it is not really sucking, it is breathing, this is what he is about, breathing her in. Seeking blindly the place where he can breathe her in. There are different zones in her thigh. She feels herself becoming something he can breathe. That moment is approaching. His gasping mouth is at the edge of her Sloggi Basic midi briefs. The fancy edge. Over it now. The fine mesh material of the briefs is like a filter to his breathing. She must become fine, microscopic, molecular, if he is to breathe her in through the fabric. The feel of his mouth, her eyes are closed now, it is easier for her to believe she is nothing, to believe she is something he can breathe, with her eyes closed. But she is not there yet. She is not nothing yet. He cannot breathe her yet. She feels his mouth through the fabric of her Sloggi Basic midi briefs. She feels the press of his mouth. She feels the crunch of her pubic hair in his mouth, through the fine filter of her Sloggi Basic midi briefs. There are pores in the fabric. The pores are stretching. Her eyes are closed. She knows the pores are stretching. She can feel the sucking of his mouth. It is not gentle any more. It is sucking. He is trying to suck her through the fabric of her Sloggi Basic midi briefs. She imagines her pubic hair being drawn by the power of his sucking mouth through the pores in the fabric of her Sloggi Basic midi briefs. Each individual pubic hair will find its own pore. She is close to the point where she will become something he can breathe. The pan. The flame under the pan. Let it catch. Let it burn. Let it. Her eyes are closed. He lifts her. She helps him. She makes an arch of her body, freeing the Sloggi Basic midi briefs, so that he can pull them down her legs. She knows to keep her legs together now. This is the point at which it helps to keep the legs together. The pan. She feels the air on her exposure. She feels the air welcome her exposure. She wants to part her legs now. It is not the time to keep her legs together now. The air. She wants to feel the air all over her now. She wants to feel the air on her, wants to feel it entering her. She feels the air must enter her so that she can become air, become one with the air, become something he can breathe. And he is trying to breathe her again. He is trying to breathe her in. He is taking big gulping lungfuls of her. He is inhaling her now. She has her eyes closed and she has become something he can breathe. She opens her eyes and looks down at his head. She sees his head. She sees her legs bent on either side of his head. She pulls her knees back and up. He is breathing her in. She is nothing and he is breathing her in. But it is crazy. She is a solid body. A body. She can see her body. She can see her legs. She can see his head. She can smell onions cooking. He has found the place where he can breathe her in. And now it is not about breathing. His head comes away from the place where he can breathe her in. He does not look her in the eyes. She has her eyes open but he doesn't look for her there. With her eyes open it is not about breathing. She is looking at his cock. It is about the bigness and the stiffness of his cock. This is for her. This is hers. It is about getting that bigness and stiffness inside her. That is what they must do. They both know this. It is what they do. They help each other do it. He is working her clitoris with his fingers. It is about this. It is about him working her clitoris with his fingers as they work the bigness and the stiffness of his cock into her. It is about her pulling his fingers away from her clitoris. She does not want that now. She wants the bigness and the stiffness inside her, all the way inside her. As far as it will go. It is about her pulling on his buttocks to get it all the way inside her. It is about feeling her eyelids pull back as it goes all the way inside her. This motion of her eyelids is minute. But it happens. Her eyes bulge. She feels it. It is about him looking her in the eye as she feels this. It is about him at last looking her in the eye. It is about her knowing that he is not afraid of her now. It is about the moment he looks her in the eye, her eyes widening as she feels the bigness and stiffness go all the way inside her, her giving him this widening of her eyes, letting him see it, not turning from him, him seeing it, him not being afraid to see it, him not being afraid. His mouth finds her earlobe. They do not need to look one another in the eye any more. They have looked one another in the eye. They have dared to do it at the moment when the bigness and stiffness is all the way inside her. They do not need to keep looking in the eye. She can look down at the bodies. This is something physical. This is a thing about bodies. This is a thing created by bodies. There comes a point where the bodies take over. It is not about her. It is not about him. It is something between their bodies. It is a thing created by bodies. It is impersonal. She is part of it. But it is not about her. It is her body panting. It is her body sweating. It is her body making that noise. It is her body. She closes her eyes. It is her body. Her body. There are no bodies. They have no bodies. There is only the thing created by bodies. She is no more. She is nothing. She is part of a thing created by bodies. He breathes her. Breathe me. He breathes her. This is how it breathes. The thing created by bodies. This is the sound of it breathing. This is the rhythm of it breathing. It sobs as it breathes. It uses her to sob as it breathes. She is the part of it that sobs as it breathes. It sobs. It sobs. Through her it sobs. She is it sobs. She is the sobs of the thing created by bodies. By his, by hers, by their bodies. He. He is it groans. He is it shakes. He is the part of the thing created by bodies that shakes.

The onions, she thinks.

She looks on the floor to where her Sloggi Basic midi briefs lie.

Figure-hugging briefs with fancy elastication at the waist and legs. Lined gusset. 95% cotton, 5% Lycra elastane.

19. Blue Hawk Plaster Coving 127x2000mm

He is lying in bed, eyes open, looking at the room. It's where the walls meet the ceiling that holds his attention. The coving. He has a way of looking at the coving, always has, it is a game he has always played. He divides it into sections, holds a section in his gaze, locks on to it. Then moves his gaze to another section, the section next to it. He goes around the room like this, travels the coving in sections. How long he holds each section is decided by something beyond his control. It is a pulse. It is something mechanical within him.

The coving is plain. The age of the house you would expect a more elaborate moulding-style cornice. But the flat is a recent conversion. Relatively. This coving was put up then, at the time of the conversion, ten fifteen twenty years ago, he does not know for sure. It is before he bought the flat. Maybe he can work it out, how long ago it was, maybe he knows and it is just that he has forgotten. He can go back to the deeds. There must be papers somewhere. He feels sure he knew and has forgotten. He knows that other people remember such things. Julia, for instance. The cornices in the living room are fancier. All the same the coving here holds his attention. Its smooth uniformity draws and holds his gaze. He cannot take his eyes off it.

He has repaired this coving. A part of it came away. He pulled it off. It broke in his hand and crumbled plaster dust onto the bed. The bit that came away was the section over the bed, over their pillows, the section he sees when he looks straight up. That is the section he replaced. He took the broken strip to Homebase, a part of it at least. He enjoys the trips to Homebase. There is purpose and congregation. It is something they do together, he and Julia. To take the strip of broken coving, to hold it next to the strips there, to find the right size, to pull out a length, it is far more than they need. To feel its serious gypsum weight. To consider the alternatives. The fancy mouldings, which though fake are more in keeping with the age of the building. To hear Julia say, Maybe we should replace the whole thing. To hear her say, I like that one, while she points out a Victorian replica. To say himself, It's polystyrene. To weigh the material in his hand. To find it flimsy and weightless and to reject it. But to be tempted all the same. This is what he enjoys. To stand in the vast warehouse, the place of concrete and ash block, amidst the aisles and shelves and milling people, comparing coving. To stand there picturing himself pulling down the coving in the bedroom, using a chisel or a screw driver or some such prising tool to pull down the coving in the bedroom, the plain coving that has started to come away. To picture himself replacing it with the flimsy tat in his hand. To know all the time that he will never do this. To know that he will reject the flimsy tat. That they are playing with the idea of the fancy fake moulding. That there is something ironic and pleasurable in all of this. That they are closer for it, that the irony has brought them closer. That they have shared a moment of perfect understanding. This is what he enjoys about the trips to Homebase.

Blue Hawk Plaster Coving 127x2000mm
- *Suits any room style*
- *Covers unsightly cracks*
- *Does not shrink or expand*
- *Provides a smooth quality finish*
- *Decorative feature between ceilings and walls*
- *Ideal for large rooms*

He is used to seeing the room like this. Whenever he can't sleep, he plays this game of dividing up the coving, of going around the room in sections. He likes to see if he can detect the length of coving he replaced. It satisfies him that he can't.

It used to be the room seemed alien at night. The streetlight glow through the curtains, red tinged from the radio alarm's LED numerals, transformed it into something he could not recognise, somewhere that is not his home. But now, tonight, to see it in this aspect is comfortingly familiar. He feels he belongs here. It is the day lit room that is alien.

Julia lies next to him. He is not sure whether she is asleep. He thinks she is.

The fucking helped. The fucking helped a lot. The coving helps. But whatever he gets from the fucking and the coving does not last.

Putting the coving in the Homebase trolley, steering it through the aisles, it is like something out of Buster Keaton or Laurel and Hardy or something. It is slapstick. The way the overhanging length swings and bashes into things, his shins, the backs of other people's legs, aisle-end displays. It is far more than they need but you cannot buy it in any shorter lengths. The comedy of it is another thing that brings them closer.

He knows where the Di Beradino classic is. He's thinking about it. He wants to go to it. He wants to open it and look inside. He is at the same time frightened of doing this. He thinks it might be a little weird, this need of his to handle the briefcase. More than a little weird. He needs to handle the things inside it too, the Benjys napkin, the Snoopy ring binder. It is more the things inside it. It is more the Snoopy ring binder. He divides the coving into sections, mentally, with his gaze. He does this to stop himself going to the Di Beradino classic. To control his need. It scares him, this need of his. Where did it come from? He never used to have such a need. It is also the briefcase but it is more the things inside it. The coving helps. He wishes he had not taken the Snoopy ring binder. It might be important to whoever needs to understand why a young Japanese assuming she is Japanese student tried to fling herself to the four corners of the earth in front of an oncoming tube train. The police, for example. Or more importantly her family. Perhaps it is better they do not understand. Perhaps it is better it is left a mystery to them. But no, he knows they have a right to understand, to attempt to understand. It is their right and he has taken it from them. He feels great remorse. He feels shame. The heat of an unseen blush ignites his skin. He feels himself start to sweat. He has done a terrible thing. Not just because it is weird. It is a violation. He has no right to the Snoopy ring binder. He wishes he could find a way to give it back to the family. To return it, somehow, to the authorities. I picked this up by mistake, he would have to say. I think it might be important. Obviously as soon as I realised my mistake... He will leave the sentence unfinished. It is better if he leaves the sentence unfinished. But he finds it hard to imagine any honest mistake that could have made him pick up the Snoopy ring binder.

He thinks about whether he will do the same thing with the Benjys napkin. He imagines tracking down the girl in the DO NOT ANGER THE GODS T-shirt. He imagines her face when he gives her back the Benjys napkin. I had no right to take this, he will say. I committed a terrible wrong when I took this. I will not rest until you take it back. It is yours by rights. He will go on in this vein for some time, he feels. For emphasis. To make sure she understands. And also to insist. He does not know how else to insist. It's all right, she will say. I don't want it. You can keep it, she will say. Whatever, she will say. Everyone says whatever these days. He begins to find it hysterically funny, this idea of tracking down the girl in the DO NOT ANGER THE GODS T-shirt. He knew all along that it was funny but now he is beginning to find it hysterically so.

He begins to shake in silent, hysterical laughter. The bed shakes.

He is afraid of waking Julia. Or disturbing her. He does not know if she is asleep. He tries to stop himself shaking. He is afraid that he will not be able to keep the laughter silent. He is afraid that something loud will come from him. It might be laughter. It might be something else. He gets out of bed.

He finds that he wants to understand. Why she wanted to fling herself to the four corners of the earth in front of the oncoming train. He needs to understand this. He has as much right as anyone to understand this. That is why he took the Snoopy ring binder. That is why he gets out of bed. It has nothing to do with waking or not waking Julia who may or may not be asleep. He finds he does not care if he wakes Julia. It will be more complicated if he wakes her. But it does not matter. Not compared to his need, his right, he would put it that strongly, to understand why the Japanese if she was Japanese student killed herself in front of him.

He moves through the lambent dark of the bedroom. The sections of coving dance in front of him in the darkness. He is not looking at them but they are dancing for him still. They want to go with him. It is a stilted dance. They want to understand too. They have a right to understand.

He handles the door carefully. He hears Julia stir in the bed behind him, rearranging herself under the duvet. So she is not asleep? Perhaps it's just a coincidence. He looks back towards the bed. It takes a moment for him to realise she is lying on her front. That the dark shape he can see is the back of her head. He cannot say what he thought it was. He cannot say why his pulse quickened, why he felt something approaching terror. It is not because he is afraid of waking her. He can deal with the complications of her waking. It is because he did not know for a moment what he was looking at. He could not make sense of the back of her head. He expected a face. He expected the face of the woman that shares his bed. He feels he has a right to expect that face, and to expect a lot from that face, what with the fucking on the sofa earlier. That is still fresh in his mind. He remembers it in his body too. In every part of his body. At the very least he expected a face, with features, all the features in place, eyes nose mouth at the very least. What he did not expect was a blank space, featureless, senseless and terrifying.

20. The Xpelair integral timer remote switch operated extract fan

He switches on the light in the bathroom. The Xpelair kicks in. He is shocked by the light and by the noise of the Xpelair. He closes the bathroom door. He thinks for a long time about locking the door. Locking the bathroom door is not something they do, not even when taking a crap. They do not leave the door open but neither do they lock it. Were he to lock the door, which is what he wants, let's say he locks it and Julia gets up and tries the door and finds it locked. That would be a difficult thing, a complication too far. That would take some explaining. He would have to have his story ready for that.

He locks the door.

He has the Di Beradino classic. There is no need to worry on that score. He has it.

Theirs is one of those tiny windowless bathrooms, a closed minimal space, a builder's afterthought. He is sealed in with the light and the singing din of the Xpelair. He knows that the fan will be audible in the bedroom, even with the doors between closed. If she is awake she will hear it. She will know he is in here. Why should he not be in here? It is a different noise that she will hear. She will hear a rumbling. It is the vibration of plasterboard that she will hear. The thought occurs to him that it is the vibrations caused by the Xpelair that shook down the length of coving. She will hear a distant, low rumbling. She will find it hard to believe it is the noise of the Xpelair because it will seem too distant, it will not seem to be coming from the next room, but from a deep subterranean chamber. Even so, she will know it for what it is. She will know that he is in there. Maybe, if she is awake, she will take a glance at the clock when she hears the Xpelair kick in. She'll take another look at the clock when she feels him get back into bed. He can imagine her doing this.

- *Single speed extract fans.*
- *Comprehensive range to suit a wide range of installations.*
- *Comprehensive range of ancillaries available.*
- *Lubricated for life motors fitted with a thermal cut out.*
- *BEAB approved.*
- *Conforms to Building Regulations Part F1*
- *2 year guarantee (UK - ONLY).*
- *Export customers see your local distributor.*

The Xpelair is on a timer switch. You have five minutes or so more of the noise, sometimes he thinks it goes on forever, after you switch out the light.

He lifts up the lid of the toilet and sits down. He's wearing soft boxers and a Muji V-neck grey T-shirt. He does not pull the boxers down. He has not come here for that.

He sets the Di Beradino classic on his lap. It digs into his legs and is cold on his legs. His body temperature is high. It is partly the remorse and the shame that he has recently come from. He is anyway one of those people who heats up at night and who cannot stand to be hot.

He has not showered since the fucking on the sofa. He is a little bit sweaty and comey. The come has dried but he can still smell it. He will shower in the morning. He wants to shower now but the noise of the shower will certainly wake Julia. Besides, this is a thing they do, this is a part of their relationship, this not showering after, this wallowing in the smell and the grubbiness of what they have done. It will seem significant if he showers. It will seem like an insult, almost. She will hear the shower and she will be hurt.

He wants to shower but he does not want to hurt her.

She cooked the meal for him in her bathrobe. The onions are burnt, she said laughing. She laughed as she threw them away. She can worry about things then laugh about the things that have worried her. He values this ability in her. They ate in bedwear and robes. He sleeps in boxers and a T-shirt. Tonight it is a Muji T-shirt, which strikes him as ironic or significant or something.

It being a Japanese brand. Julia sleeps in a light sweatsuit. They did not talk about what they had done. They never do. They did not attempt to explain what it meant, though he feels she wants to ask him something. She has something on her mind, he feels sure. That is why she is lying awake. She is waiting to ask him about something that he will be reluctant to explain. Or unable.

He is now conBarryd she is awake.

His hands are shaking as he opens the briefcase. The sound of the Xpelair is vibrating in his hands, throughout the whole of him. His bones transmit the vibrations into the Snoopy ring binder as he takes it out.

He cannot control the shaking as he handles the Snoopy ring binder. It is the vibrations from the Xpelair is one way of explaining it.

With one hand he moves the briefcase onto the floor. Now he lays the Snoopy ring binder flat on his lap. Its vinyl skin cold against his own skin. He runs his fingers over its vinyl smoothness, as though he can absorb the understanding he needs in this way. He is seeking out that thing with the different colours, the texture and gradient of the inks. The touch of the inks satisfies. He is ready. He opens the Snoopy ring binder. There are about ten or so pages of A4 ruled feint. That word feint actually comes into his mind at this moment, though he has no idea what it means. Do they mean faint? If so it is no big deal. It is prepunched paper with four holes. Probably from a bumper refill pad. Probably from Rymans or Woolworths. He has an image of the girl buying the paper. She is over here in a foreign country. She has to buy paper. She is baffled by the lines. She is baffled by the word feint. They do not think of foreigners when they use words like feint. He thinks of everyone. He is a marketing man. It is his job to think of everyone. The lines are no use to her. The word feint is no use to her. She writes in Japanese. He recognises the characters as Japanese. He is certain about this. The Japanese characters read from top to bottom. Every page is full on both sides with tight neat closely packed Japanese characters reading top to bottom. She writes over the lines. She ignores the lines. He knows her writing is neat even though he cannot understand it. So he knows this about her, that she had neat writing. It is all he knows about her and he clings to it. He hugs the open Snoopy ring binder to his chest, pushing the neat but incomprehensible Japanese characters into the fabric of his Muji grey V-neck T-shirt. There is a change in the quality of the vibrations he feels from the Xpelair. He knows that he will make the noise, the noise he had been afraid of making in bed. It comes, the noise. It is not laughter. It is the noise caused by the vibrations inside him. He is a sounding box for the vibrations. He cannot control it. It shakes him. He squeezes his eyes shut and lets the noise work through him.

21. The Philips AJ3120 radio alarm clock

She feels the dip as he gets back in. She checks the red numerals of the Philips AJ3120 radio alarm clock. 03:29. Jesus.

The glowing recto-form numerals seem enormous in the dark.

She watches 03:29 change to 03:30. She feels there is something decisive in the symmetry of this.

Rob?

Yes?

Are you all right?

Yes.

They are voices in the dark. They do not attempt to see each other. She is looking at the clock. He is looking, she does not know where he is looking but she knows he is not attempting to see her.

Why were you crying?

Crying? There is a fraudulent snag in his voice she notices.

When you came in tonight, you were crying. You had your head in your hands crying. We haven't talked about it.

It was nothing.

It can't be nothing.

Just. Just a shitty day, that's all.

Your first day.

It's all right. It's nothing. Something really minor.

Tell me.

There is a pause. She watches the clock to measure the pause. It seems 03:30 will last forever. They are stuck on 03:30.

It's just I was sitting in on this guy taking in-bound calls. He was, you know... I just didn't like him. A wanker. This lady phoned up about her flat roof.

03:31.

It was really sad. Her husband had just died. You know, and he was actually quite horrible to her. I felt.

That's terrible.

I just felt, it wasn't good for the company, the way he treated her. It's bad for the brand. You know? Everything has an impact on the brand. She'll talk to people. Word will get round. She could even go to the press.

And you care about her feelings.

I suppose I do. I think someone should write to her and apologise.

You could.

It doesn't have to be me but someone should.

It might make you feel better if you did it.

I'm all right. I'm going to be all right. No more... of that. Nonsense.

You don't have to be afraid. Of crying.

03:32. It is the time to turn away from the clock. It is the time to offer him something more than her voice. It is the time to be more to him than a voice in the darkness. She nestles up to him, chin finding shoulder, chin probing nestling snuggling into shoulder.

I was worried about you.

No need to be.

Her hand feels momentous in the dark as she moves it to his face, to feel his face, to discover with her touch the fresh wetness on his face.

Oh, Rob. Oh, Rob, she says.

She hears the fan in the bathroom cut out. The silence startles her.

22. The Nike Air Zoom Elite running shoes

He runs. He shadowboxes. He puts on spurts. He high-steps. He runs. He puts on orange and white Nike Air Zoom Elites and runs.

He has always done this, for as long as he can remember. It is not something he is going to be deterred from.

The new day is a fine day. The new day encourages him. He is still grubby from the fucking on the sofa last night. And from the tears. The tears have made him grubby too. The tears are dry now but he still feels the vestiges of them pulling at his face. He will run from that, from all of it. He will sweat new hot sweat. And he will shower. The new day gives him hope.

FAST AND RESPONSIVE.

ADD TOGETHER THE BEST ELEMENTS OF THE SPAN AND SKYLON AND WHAT DO YOU GET? THE AIR ZOOM ELITE: BUILT FOR DISTANCE YET LIGHT AND FAST.

He can almost believe it never happened. Each day is its own universe. The only thing he is carrying over from yesterday is the corney grubbiness and the saline contraction of his face skin. These are things he can wash off. He does not feel the need to have the Di Beradino with him. It would be ridiculous to see a running man carry a briefcase but he does not feel the need to do it. He is over his need. Whatever it was it was a thing of yesterday. And every morning he runs from the day before. He gets up early to escape the day before.

His route is fifty percent road running. The Air Zoom Elites can handle this. He can run on the pavement forever in his Air Zoom Elites.

A FULL LENGTH, LOW PROFILE 'ZOOM' AIR BAG MAKES FOR A VERY LIGHT, RESPONSIVE HEEL TO TOE RIDE. A SCULPTED MIDFOOT SHANK AIDS TRANSITION AND SUPPORT, WHILE DUAL DENSITY CORRECTS MILD OVER PRONATION.

It is fifty percent pavements but it also takes in Queen's Wood. This is the part of the run he enjoys the most. The pavement running is fine but it is burdened with purpose. The purpose of it is to get here, amongst the trees. He likes to run between the trees. He likes to run on the track, the pounded earth track, the softer feel of the track. The Air Zoom Elites can handle the transition. Sometimes the track is high, he is above the wood. Sometimes it takes him down into the heart of the wood. There are places where a stream dissects the path. He has to leap over the stream's ditch. It is uplifting to leap in this way. It is an easy leap, he takes it in his stride. He even forms that expression in his mind as he does it. He appreciates the opportunity to use a metaphorical expression literally. Such expressions come to life, he believes, when their meaning is literal and real.

It is a privilege to be in the woods at this time of the day. He almost has the woods to himself. This is the reward for getting up an hour earlier than he needs to.

The only person he sees is a middle-aged man walking his dog. He sees this man every morning. He is always properly dressed, sometimes even smart, school-teacher smart. Today he wears a brown corduroy jacket and tweed trousers. Rob can tell whether he is early or late by where he is in the wood when he sees the man. Rob has him down as a school teacher, or a retired school teacher. He is old enough to be retired. Something about him must remind Rob of a teacher he had at school. He thinks of a certain history teacher. Something about the angle and height of the forehead, and the weight of the glasses. He sees this man every morning. They do not acknowledge each other. Rob used to acknowledge the man but he never got any acknowledgement back, so now he has stopped. He cannot think why the man will not return his acknowledgement. Except once, when they were approaching each other, Rob sneezed and a viscous shower of phlegm came out of his nose. The man was some way off and none of it reached him. In fact it went all over Rob. It was Rob who had to deal with it, though of course he just ignored it. But he knows the man saw it.

The man's dog is a spaniel. It is mostly white with brown ears and brown tail and brown patches on the body. It is always eager and friendly and acknowledging. It is always pleased to see

Rob. The dog is excited by his running, he knows that is all it is. But Rob always smiles to himself as he runs past, as soon as he is past them, at the dog who acknowledges him and the owner who doesn't.

He thinks on balance the man is not a teacher. He has him down now as a writer. Maybe he is famous. Maybe that is where the not acknowledging comes from. Maybe he is a great and famous writer. He is self-absorbed. He comes to Queen's Wood with his dog to absorb himself in his thoughts. He is a writer or he pursues some other solitary occupation. He could be a mathematician. He's been working for years on an intractable mathematical theorem. He has made it his life's work to prove the unprovable. In that case, Rob can forgive him for being distracted. Or a composer. Something like that. Or maybe the man has Asperger's Syndrome. You hear a lot about that these days.

GOING THE DISTANCE? AN OPEN FOREFOOT PROVIDES ROOM FOR YOUR FOOT TO EXPAND ON LONGER RUNS. ENJOY THE RIDE.

He does not think about the man for long. The running opens him up. The running expands him.

23. The Flexi Classic 1 small dog 5m retractable dog lead

Come on Frederick, he thinks but does not say as the runner passes them. He does not want to speak in the presence of the runner. Even to call out to his dog. He cannot explain why he has got it into his head to hate the runner so much. To resent him would be reasonable and maybe it started with resentment. The runner is a trespasser. The woods are his alone at this time of the day. The hour is his alone. The runner is unwelcome. But to hate him so much? To feel such rage at the sight of him? He does not quite understand it but he is not willing to do anything about it. His rage comforts him.

Frederick is off the lead, the Flexi Classic 1. The dog runs ahead, veers off into the trees, circles back and catches up. This is his pattern. Or he just trots alongside. Quite often he is happy to trot alongside. There is no need for the lead in the woods. The lead would only get tangled around the trees.

The cord is coiled inside the plastic handle. The handle is husky and light when the cord is fully extended but now it has a satisfying weight in his hand.

Maybe he hates the runner's youth. He feels that is possible. The young today are without fear or shame. At the root of his hatred is envy. That's all. He knows this. So many people make him cross. So many things.

Of course, he knows what it is really about.

Come on Frederick, he says, out loud, now that the runner is long gone.

He will see him again today, Fitzpatrick. And it will get nasty again. Fitzpatrick will threaten to tell Sheila. He will demand money. How could it have come to this? How could he have let it come to this? The man was a bloody squaddie. This is what happens when you fraternise with the lower ranks.

He smiles sarcastically at the word. Fraternise. How could he have allowed it to start?

He will get the money. He has decided he will get the money. Today he will get the money, before he sees Fitzpatrick. He has already moved the money over. He has already taken steps. Sheila need never know anything about it. It is better that he does this. She will never know. She leaves it all to him anyhow, the money side of things.

It is because it will be so easy that he has resisted doing it. She trusts him. And he will be trampling on her trust. He is not without honour. Despite all he has allowed to happen and all that is yet to happen, he feels that he is not without honour. It grieves him to betray her trust. But it is better than she finds out.

But how can he be sure it will be the end of it? Can he really be sure Fitzpatrick will let it go at that?

He has to admit Fitzpatrick scares him. He has to admit that it is because Fitzpatrick scares him that he let it start. It was his fear that drew him to Fitzpatrick. Still draws him. It is as if he has condensed his fear, all the fear he is capable of feeling, into one man. At least it is contained. As for the rest of it, it is shameful and humiliating and that is why he hates the runner. Because he sees in the runner a man who has not yet been humiliated. And that is why he envies the young. These days there is no shame in such things. These days the young live without shame. They talk about such things openly. They celebrate such things.

One thing is for sure, Sheila must never know about that side of it. There is no way she would be able to understand that side of it.

Come on Frederick, he calls. It is time to fix the lead on the dog's collar. It is time for the cord to unwind, for the handle to become a husk in his hand again.

24. Whole Earth Organic Corn Flakes

She is dressed by the time Rob gets back from his run. Today she has chosen a skirt and a light weight jersey. She worries that she will be too hot in the jersey. But she wants to wear the skirt and the jersey goes well with the skirt. She stands in the living room eating a bowl of Whole Earth Organic Corn Flakes, holding the bowl with one hand, spooning the cornflakes with the other. She is careful not to dribble.
Light, Crisp & Tasty
NOTHING ARTIFICIAL • GLUTEN FREE
A delicious organic cereal made with the finest organic ingredients
She stands and eats and watches the breakfast news on the TV. There is coverage of an earthquake in Turkey. She hears the bathroom fan and the shower's clatter. She watches silent scenes of devastation. She has the TV on mute. She is listening to the shower.

She has always eaten cornflakes for breakfast, ever since childhood. Then it was Kellogg's. Now it is Whole Earth Organic. Now the milk is skimmed and she no longer adds sugar. She doesn't miss the sugar or the full-fat milk or the taste of Kellogg's. She is an adult. She is rational. She knows that Whole Earth Organic Corn Flakes with skimmed milk and no sugar are better for her. She is careful about what she eats. Her body is the shape and size she wants it to be. She worries too about pesticides and poisons and genetic modification. She worries about cancer and Alzheimer's and about disease in general and about ageing and mortality and death. She worries about her mother. She feels better eating Whole Earth Organic Corn Flakes, no sugar, skimmed milk. She worries less about those things with this bowl in her hand. She feels she is doing more to keep them at bay. She congratulates herself on how little she misses her infantile tastes, on how delicious she believes Whole Earth Organic Corn Flakes to be. It is true that she knows she would get a certain kind of comfort from eating a bowl of Kellogg's, sprinkled liberally with white refined sugar, doused in full fat milk. But she gets another kind of comfort from the bowl she is eating from now. She has chosen this comfort over the other one.

At Whole Earth we believe that breakfast is the most important meal of the day. Corn Flakes is not only delicious but a healthy way to start your day.

The shower stops. Rob comes in towel-drying his hair. He is naked. There is nothing more natural than his walking in naked while she watches the TV fully clothed. The thrill she feels is not sexual it is pride. Rob stands naked rubbing a towel through his hair watching the TV as bodies and injured people are lifted from wreckage. She takes pride in his body.

What's happened to the sound? he asks.

It's on mute.

Why? There is a tone to the question that she recognises. It is mocking but it recognises that she will not be offended by the mocking, that she will understand and even enjoy it. It signals all that there is between them. It is like him standing there naked towel-drying his hair.

She answers with a shrug.

Where's the remote?

He finds the remote and the TV begins to speak to them.

Collapsing buildings are still impeding rescue work. The question being asked is why have so many buildings been damaged in what seismologists have described as a light tremor. Locals blame corrupt officials who they say have failed to enforce construction regulations.

Julia watches a small child being carried on a stretcher. She watches rescue workers crowd round the child, a boy it is. Such images of the injured always strike her as overly intimate and intrusive. Clothes are stripped away. Wounds are exposed. The injured are left no dignity. Julia eats her Whole Earth Organic Corn Flakes. The milk seems thin. She longs for sugar. She longs for the taste of her childhood, the taste of Kellogg's.

Out of the devastation, one small miracle. This three-year-old boy was trapped for twelve hours. His mother, father and three sisters were not so lucky. No one has yet told him that he is the sole surviving member of his family.

Rob leaves the room, towelling his hair.

25. The Tetley teabag

She puts the Tetley teabag in the Twirl mug and waits for the kettle to boil.

Naturally rich in antioxidants…

She has filled the kettle although she only wants one cup. The filling of the kettle is for the others. She stands and waits. There is nothing worse than going away and coming back to find someone else has had your water. Even though you have put your Tetley teabag in your Twirl mug they do this. It is a way of staking a claim. It is a marker. But it is not enough. They take the water. They do not even think, when the kettle boils, to put water in the Twirl mug, for the person who has filled the kettle, who has obviously gone away for the moment while the kettle boils, the kettle takes a long time to boil they know this. No, the leaving of the mug is not enough. She must stand guard over the boiling kettle. They force her to do this. It is annoying when someone takes your water, but it does not crush her. The best thing is when she comes to the kitchen and finds someone else has just boiled the kettle. They have boiled the kettle and taken their water and left the rest for the others, for her. It is because she knows how good this feels that she always fills the kettle. Coming and finding the kettle with water in it, she knows all she has to do is press the button on the kettle, it will pop back up immediately so recently has the water boiled. It is a good feeling, a happy moment. She feels a little grim and mean standing guard over the boiling kettle like this, but it is something she does.

The kettle boils. She lifts the kettle off its stand. It is one of those plastic cordless kettles that lift clear of a circular stand. She has submerged hypnosis-susceptible memories of metal kettles.

As always in the moment before she pours the boiling water, she has the sense that the Twirl mug will melt.

Tetley assures a perfect cup of tea every time! Our popular soft packs are resealable and more compact, making them easier to handle and store. Tetley Tea is a rich source of flavonoid antioxidants. The antioxidants found in tea, fruit and vegetables form an important part of a healthy diet.

The water hits the mug and she expects the mug to melt, something about the colour purple, its association with chocolate, and this is a Twirl mug. But it doesn't melt.

The water darkens instantly. She waits to push down the spoon. There is something to be said for watching the darkness thicken throughout the mug. For allowing it to happen at its own speed, without intercession. There is a temptation to press down with the spoon but this would be a mistake, a wasted opportunity. There are moments of natural slowness in life and they must be relished. This is one of them. The teabag must be allowed to float and leech. But also there comes a point when the pleasure you are taking in the slowness of the moment, its tendril-delicacy, becomes tinged with guilt and the urge to press down with the spoon becomes too great. Sandra feels this. She is feeling the urge become too much for her. The slowness of the moment begins to make her anxious. She is afraid that someone will come into the kitchen space and spoil her enjoyment of watching the Tetley teabag infuse. The pleasure she is taking is loaded with its own destruction.

She presses down with the teaspoon. She squeezes the antioxidant-rich flavour out of the Tetley teabag. You do not leave the teabag in there long after this. The squeezing always signals the end. She opens the bin in readiness. She has the sodden Tetley teabag on the spoon. It overhangs the edges. There is something louche about the shape it forms. She ferries it over to the bin and drops it. Her timing is perfect. There are no drips.

She adds the milk, semi-skimmed of course, everyone drinks semi-skimmed these days. She remembers the tea Nan used to make with sterilised milk. She almost believes she can remember the taste. She used to have it sweet with lots of sugar. But it was the sterilised milk that made it taste special. She thinks perhaps one day she would like to buy some sterilised milk and make herself a cup of tea like that. She wonders if it is something she will do when she is old.

She adds a Canderel and stirs. She has Canderel. That's all that's left of those sweet teas she Nan used to make.

She carries the mug out of the kitchen space towards her workstation. She has to go along one small length of corridor before she reaches the sales and marketing area. He is coming towards her, the new one, Rob. She wants to smile for him, she has this thing about smiling, but she wants to smile for him. But the wanting to smile is too conscious. A smile cannot be manufactured like this. Not if it is to be a natural smile. And she will give only natural smiles. She cannot make herself smile. They have passed each other and she has not smiled. But then neither has he. She does not look back. She does not know whether he looks back. She has the feeling he does. She hopes he does.

26. The IBM ThinkVision L170P flat panel monitor

The Di Beradino classic is under his desk, under the Unifor i Satelliti S200. He knows the briefcase is there and he knows what it contains but he is not anxious about its contents. Specifically the Snoopy ring binder and the Benjys napkin but also his current paperback and a banana. He has not made the leap to two bananas. The comb-bound *Welcome to Diamond Life* document is no longer in the briefcase. He has that on the desk. There's also a phone on the desk and a laminated card explaining how to use the phone, in particular the voicemail facility. Also on his desk are the keyboard, mouse, mousepad and monitor for his PC. The processor is under the desk, on the opposite side to the Di Beradino classic. The PC is an IBM ThinkCentre M Series. It is black. More and more these days computers are black. He wonders when this started happening and why. They used to be grey or maybe you would say beige, it's hard to remember now the exact shade that computers used to be. By whose decision, with whose consent, this spread of black computers? It does not anger him, but he was never consulted. And of course, he had no say in the choice of this particular computer. He is happy that the processor is out of sight.

He does not feel the need to look at the contents of the briefcase or handle them.

He has work to do. He has to turn the handles on the Unifor i Satellliti S200, adjusting the height of the desk top, there is one handle to do that and another raises the platform for his IBM ThinkVision L170P flat panel monitor. He is happy that it is flat panel. He would have chosen flat panel himself. He has to adjust his chair. There are many levers and screws on the chair that can be turned. The arms go up and down. The seat goes up and down. He must get the height of the chair right and then adjust the desk to match it. This is what he must do this morning. He has the time and the confidence to do it. Yesterday he couldn't do it. He had other things on his mind. It is impossible, on the day that you have seen someone throw themselves in front of a hurtling tube train, to think of adjusting your workplace chair.

He knows the Snoopy ring binder is in there and the napkin. It is more the Snoopy ring binder that he is aware of. He could have taken them out and left them at home. He feels he could have done this. He does not feel he needs them any more. He could easily have taken them out. It is only that he forgot to do so.

He adjusts the platform for his IBM ThinkVision L170P flat panel monitor. He has never had an independently adjustable platform for a PC monitor before. It amuses him that he is pleased to have such a feature on his desk. It is a joke. It is ironic. But at the same time, he has to admit that it is a genuine benefit. Feature, benefit. He is a marketing man. He knows that a feature alone is not enough. Every feature must have a benefit. The beauty is it's so simple. You do not want to look down at the monitor, your body does not want this. It curves your body, it curves your spine, it strains your neck, this always looking down at the monitor. Your position is better in the chair if you can look straight ahead at the monitor. Your back is straighter, you are holding your head high, you sit tall, you are proud, if you can raise the height of the monitor. It is a question of ergonomics. And psychology. Being able to change the height of your monitor whenever you wish, at a whim you might say, means that your posture is periodically refreshed. It also gives you control over your environment. These are good things. He has not had this explained to him, but he understands it and embraces it, without of course abandoning the privilege of irony.

It is satisfying to turn the handle and see the platform rise, to turn it the other way and see it drop. The action of the turning handles is smooth and seductive. It is well-engineered. It is effortless. The desk is laden with engineering to make it effortless.

At last he has the desk the way he wants it. The angle of his head as he looks at the ThinkVision is just perfect. He feels supported by his chair. The reach of his hand to the mouse is just perfect. When he moves his right hand from keyboard to mouse there is no overreaching. It is comfortable. There is no bending of the back to rest his wrists on the desk top as he types.

The computer runs XP. He has worked with XP. He is comfortable with XP.

The gentle 3D modelling of the interface reassures him. The start-up mnemonic jingle is familiar and comforting. He knows where he is with XP. The colours soothe him. He can find his way round with XP. My Documents, My Pictures, My Music, My Computer, My Network Places. He can get on to the server easily. He can access the Z drive effortlessly. He can find the customer database and open it. It runs on Microsoft Axapta. Everything runs on Microsoft Axapta, the whole company. Sales and Marketing, Financial Management, Business Planning, Human Resources. He does not have access to all these departments. But he can get into the customer database. He is familiar with Microsoft Axapta. He would even say he is comfortable with it, though he finds the grey boxy interface old-fashioned. But it is functional. He knows that is the point.

He can enter a name. Green. Emily. Emily Green. Mrs Emily Green.

She is there, her details, on the IBM ThinkVision L170P flat panel monitor in the boxy grey Microsoft Axapta interface. She is there for him.

The layout is intuitive. There is built-in user help. There are Windows commands. There is copy and paste. He shades a mouse block over her details and copies her details. This is easy for him to do. It is familiar. He is comfortable.

It is an easy thing for him to switch to Word, to switch back to the letter he has drafted in Word, to enter her details into the letter. He could use Mail Merge but he uses Word. He is more comfortable with Word.

The letter is there, on the IBM ThinkVision L170P flat panel monitor, inside the IBM ThinkCentre M Series. He can scroll up and down the letter. He can roll the wheel on the black mouse to make the letter jump. He does this. He makes the letter jump. He's not exactly reading it. He's reassuring himself that it's there. The letter is just words on a screen. It is just a potential. The letter is just an idea.

But if he drops down the file box, rolls down to print, if he sends the letter to print, it becomes real.

27. The Montblanc Meisterstück Le Grand fountain pen

He likes the weight of the pen in his hand. If you are the C.E.O. of a middle-ranking financial company, a publicly listed company, you will be called upon to sign things. You will need a pen. You will need a serious pen. You will need a Montblanc.
In times that are changing ever faster, we need things that preserve the moment.
There are more ostentatious Montblancs than the Meisterstück Le Grand. He could have chosen one from the Solitaire Royal range, the Meisterstück Solitaire Royal Le Grand for instance. Eighteen carat yellow gold set with four thousand eight hundred and ten diamonds. He can afford such a pen. But it is not about what you can or cannot afford. It is about what feels right in your grip. Compared to the Meisterstück Solitaire Royal Le Grand, his Montblanc is understated. That is the word, understated. A simple black resin pen with gold trims. He has gone for the optional signature nib, gold inlaid with platinum. It is the classic Montblanc.

He is comfortable in his status. He wants others to be comfortable too. It is a Montblanc is enough. A more ostentatious Montblanc would draw attention to his status, to his wealth, to his success. It would make others uncomfortable. He has to work with these people. But he has a sense too of what is due to him.

He knows the preconceptions these people have about Americans, the prejudice would not be putting it too strong. They would expect him to have a more ostentatious Montblanc. He is determined to show them that he is civilised. That he has an understanding and love of European culture. He talks to them of novels and movies. He even knows to call them films. He has made a point of reading English writers, though his favourite book remains *The Sheltering Sky*. He owns a signed first edition, bought from Robert Dagg Rare Books in San Francisco. He wonders if there is a connection between his love of this book and his decision to work in the insurance sector. He has worked hard to learn the names of famous Brits, celebrities, soap stars, pop stars, even some politicians. He prides himself of knowing the name of the leader of the opposition. He has taken his daughters to the Houses of Parliament. They sat in the House of Commons public gallery. He has watched football, he knows not to call it soccer, they will not catch him out making such a fundamental mistake. He has been to Stamford Bridge to watch Chelsea play live. He has opinions about the English national side, about the tactics. He only once made the mistake of calling it the UK team. He has always been a huge Monty Python fan, huge is the word he uses. He has travelled widely in Europe. He has been to Paris and Vienna and other places. Ireland. Italy. He has travelled extensively in Italy. He knows to make fun of himself, of his Americanness. The spelling. Tire instead of tyre. He is learning English words, English slang, English abuse. He surprised them all once by saying wanker. He is trying to get to the bottom of Cockney rhyming slang.

He knows that they are suspicious of him, that they did not want him, do not want him. Some of them have good reason not to want him. But he will not give them the satisfaction of confirming their prejudices. The last thing he will be is brash.

So he talks to them of civilised things. He takes enjoyment in civilised things and then shares his enjoyment of these things with them. He enjoys the opera. He loves the ENO. He takes his daughters to the British Museum, the National Gallery, the V&A, both Tates, Modern and Britain. He books to see the latest blockbuster exhibitions and takes his daughters to them. He brings these experiences into work and tries to talk about them, tries to find someone he can talk to about them. He is dismayed that no one is interested. That no one has been or intends to go to these exhibitions. That they openly express their hatred of opera. That they go instead at weekends to garden centres and DIY stores. That they prefer simply to get drunk, without even the interpolation of good food. That they will wait for the DVD. He often has the feeling that he is talking to himself. But he will not let them get away with it, he will not let them change him. He will not be brought down by them. He thinks of it as coming down to their level. He will continue to take delight in these things and to talk of them. He will continue to rebuke them with his love of culture. He will not be ashamed of it. And he is the American.

He realises he is separated from these people not by his nationality, but by his status after all. Over here they do not seem to buy into the idea that what is good for him is good for them all. That one day they could all be the guy with the Montblanc, any one of them. He thinks perhaps he should get himself a Solitaire Royal after all. It would be a way of saying fuck you, fuck you all. It hasn't come to that yet, but some days he is tempted.

For nearly one hundred years the name Montblanc has stood for the art of writing, while the snow-covered peak of Mont Blanc has symbolised the high quality status of the brand with the distinctive white star.

He is putting the cap on his Montblanc Meisterstück Le Grand fountain pen when Tony Dawson and the new guy Rob come in. He has asked them to drop by. He does not believe in sending out formal Entourage-generated invitations to be declined or accepted. He believes in asking people to drop by. He has an open door policy. He is Al to them. Not Mr Morello. Not sir. He does not need to protect himself from the people who work for him.

Though he has seen them, though his door is open, they knock as they come through.

Yep, he says.

They stand uneasily at the door, only just inside his office.

Sit down, guys. He insists on saying guys.

They sit side by side on to the Artemia Le Corbusier replica two-seater sofa.

He wishes he had not capped the pen because he wants now something to do before turning to them, before lifting his gaze to face them, some little bit of business to mark the transition. He has no wish to be rude. It is simply that he needs to gather his thoughts. He is aware that they are looking at him. He pretends to read again the letter he has just signed. He is conscious of the artificiality of what he is doing. He drops the letter.

He lifts his gaze to face them.

So, he says, what did you make of yesterday?

He watches them closely. He sees a look he does not like pass between them. There is something sarcastic in it. What the fuck is this stupid Yank talking about now? it says. It passes from Dawson to the new guy. To be fair to the new guy, he frowns it down, will not have it.

They do not answer. It seems he will have to spell it out for them.

Gina's very smart, he says.

Dawson's feigned enlightenment is overdone.

She's a very good planner, says Tony Dawson. He makes it sound like he knows what he is talking about, though there is also the suspicion that he is repeating something he has been told. The planning is always excellent from BHBY, he says.

Yeah, but those other guys. Steve and Guy. He makes it funny, the way he says this, the way he deliberately gets their names wrong.

Dave and Si. The creatives. He lets Dawson correct him. That is the whole point. There's a smile in Dawson's voice that acknowledges this. But the time has come to pay him back for that look.

Let me be honest with you, Tony. Our last campaign was a turkey.

His marketing director is squirming like he wants to go to the bathroom, though over here they say loo, he knows that. Then he realises that the man is squaring up to him on the Artemia Le Corbusier replica two-seater sofa. It's not squirming it's a shuffle of aggression. He's shuffling like a bouncer. The smell of his aggression suddenly hits Al.

Then the guy buckles. It did under-perform, he concedes.

It stank. Right, Rob?

He thinks maybe he is a little cruel to use that word now, considering the rich hormonal atmosphere.

I can't really comment. It was before my time.

He thinks it stank too.

There were lessons, says Tony Dawson. Which we have learnt.

Al nods but he doesn't mean to signal concurrence. Rather finality, decision. Power.

Here's an idea, he says. Just wanted to bounce it off you. His tone is as hard as a bouncing ball bearing.

Now it's their turn to nod and they do so in unison. A nod of submission. The opposite of his nod.

How about we put the account up for review? The whole lot. Everything. Advertising. DM. The full Monty. That should shake things up, what? he says. He enjoys overdoing the Anglicisms.

Dawson, clever Dawson, is quick to come back with, Good idea.

What do you think, Rob?

The other one nods agreement. I like a good pitch, he says. It's fun. And he's grinning like he means it.

So you'll draw up a long list? He's looking at Rob as he says this.

Yeah, we can do that for you, says Dawson, quick to muscle in, feeling the need to assert his authority.

Al smiles. He feels his smile and feels the effect of it. I want Rob to do it, he insists through his smile. I think it would be good for him.

Under my supervision, obviously. Tony Dawson is not smiling.

I want Rob to do it on his own. It'll be good for both of you. Rob gets some independence. And you, Tony, you learn the deep, sweet joy of delegation. You're the marketing director for Christ's sake. Let Rob draw up the long list.

But Rob has only been with the company for two days, not even two days. This is only his second day. The hormonal aroma thickens to a stench.

Al has the Montblanc Meisterstück Le Grand in his hand again. He points it towards Tony Dawson. He gives it a little flourish of emphasis.

That's why I want him to do it, Tony.

He doesn't hold the smile. He has seen what happens when you hold the smile too long. It stiffens. Better to hold the pen and wave the pen, to cut the air with the pen.

Dawson nods slowly, finally getting it. Al can see that he has got it at last.

28. The Unifor Progetto 25 screen system and the TAG Heuer Kirium Ti5 Men's Chronograph

He has to nip this in the bud. He has to make sure Rob understands, whatever Morello says, he has to make sure the new boy understands it the way it is.

The guy's only been here for five minutes, for crying out loud. Sure, he's got a good CV. He's got agency experience. But does he understand the business? Does he fuck. Not from the inside out.

He has to lay down the ground rules. He has to tell it like it is. This is leadership. He has to stand on one side of the Unifor Progetto 25 screen finished in grey forbo, looking down at the Unifor i Satelliti S200, at the back of the IBM ThinkVision L170P flat panel monitor, at the top of Rob's head, and he has to tell it like it is.

He has to rest his forearms on the top of the Unifor Progetto 25 screen. He has to give the screen some of his weight to take, has to lean forward so the screen supports him. There have to be ground rules. There have to be boundaries. Some of us have offices. Some of us have Unifor Progetto 25 screens. It is for the men with offices to stand over the men with Unifor Progetto 25 screens. It is for the men with offices to lay down the ground rules. This is leadership.

It is important to nip this in the bud now. This is leadership. He can do leadership. He has to do what is required.

Progetto 25 (closed spaces). Luca Meda

Partition system for contemporary work environments. Wide variety of functional spaces that never stop changing, adapting with ease to each specific need. Public areas, task zones, managerial offices, rooms for communicating. Places both open and private, protected and in constant communion with one another. Comfortable and custommade. Wall systems, freestanding panels, transparent surfaces, telescopic sliding divider elements, luminous strips, easily accessed modules for raceway installations, sliding doors in glass and side-hinged doors...

Flexible components in a unique constructive system that never stops growing.

OK, this is what you need to do.

This is what he has to say and this is what he says. It has the desired effect. It has the effect of making Rob look at him.

The first thing you need to do is get on to the AAR. Get some agency reels in. Speak to Emma Jenkins there. Tell her it's for me. Tony Dawson at Diamond Life. Mention my name. She's good Emma. She's a darling. We should be talking to top 50 agencies. Fuck the top 100. We'll start with the top 50. There's your long list there actually. With a bit of pruning. And tell her you want some wild cards in there. Maybe a regional. That'll mix it up. Or a start-up. Go through recent Campaigns and look for start-up stories. Check the lineage and if they're offshoots from top 50 agencies, no top 10, tell her we want to see the reels or the brochures or whatever they have. They may not have reels if they're start-ups.

He is running out of commands to issue but is afraid to stop talking. He does not know what will happen if he stops talking. There is a danger if he stops talking that Rob will stop looking at him. There is even a danger that Rob will say something he does not wish to hear. So he carries on talking. He has to keep talking. This is leadership.

You can do a lot of the groundwork over the internet. Pick some agencies that catch your eye. Google them. Get some contact details. I have some agency reels in my office. You can spend an hour going through those.

He really is running out of things to say now. He is going to have to start repeating himself. Whatever happens it is important that he doesn't give Rob the opportunity to look away or say anything. He has to start repeating himself.

Yeah, so start with Emma at the AAR. Tell her we'll be talking to ad agencies. Tell her we're looking at DM too. They can help us with DM as well. There won't be reels there. Not so much. You should also get on to the DMA or is it the IDM. I've got back issues of Precision Marketing.

What he hates is the way his mouth is drying up as he speaks. What he also hates is the way he can smell his own body odour as he speaks. The way he knows his breath stinks too. He feels this undermines his authority. This is something that makes him want to stop talking and go back to his office and hide from all of them, from Morello, from Rob, from Sandra, particularly from Sandra, not so much from Ian and Geoff but definitely from Sandra. This is something that makes his palms sweat. It makes him want to be in the Feathers.

You should spend some time going through them. Concentrate on the big players. Find out about awards. There are awards there too. It might be worth looking into that. I can get you a number for the AAR. I'll email you a number for the AAR.

The fucker cuts in. He hasn't even finished saying what he's got to say and the fucker cuts in. Tony, he says. He asked me to do it.

You realise I'll have the final say, don't you? He wishes he hadn't said this but he has. It's too late. He's said it.

So now Rob's looking away from him, intent on his IBM ThinkVision L170P flat panel monitor.

First he cuts in, now he cuts me out.

He has to do something.

He decides the thing he will do is look at his watch. His TAG Heuer Kirium Ti5 Men's Chronograph.

Listen, he will say as he looks at his watch.

But something happens as he moves his arm to look at the TAG Heuer Kirium Ti5. He moves his arm in a certain way. It is a brandishing of the arm. Does he try to make this movement of the arm threatening? He cannot believe that is what's in his mind. The thing is, however, in this brandishing of the arm, the watch, the TAG Heuer Kirium Ti5 Men's Chronograph, catches on the top of the Unifor Progetto 25 screen finished in grey forbo. The screen is solid. There is no danger of knocking the screen over but it makes a cracking sound. It sounds like he has cracked the face of the TAG Heuer Kirium Ti5. How this is possible he doesn't know but his heart is going like the tenth of a second hand as he checks the face. You can imagine how his heart must be going.

Not a scratch. He says this. Not a scratch, he says.

That's good. I'm glad, says Rob, but without really convincing anyone that he means it.

A few of us are going down the Feathers at lunchtime. Tony hears himself say this and wonders what is going on, what the fuck is going on.

Is it that time? I've just got a few things to do. You know, with the long list and everything.

And now he blows me out.

Don't take the brown nosing too far.

Leadership.

Yeah, well, I might see you in there. Just got to write a few things up while they're fresh in my mind.

You know where to find us.

Feathers.

He pats the top of the Unifor Progetto 25 screen then fingertip touches the unscratched face of his TAG Heuer Kirium Ti5 Men's Chronograph as he nods and moves away. He tries to make himself weightless as he moves away.

29. The Securicor security box

So it is that time. He seriously had not realised it was that time. He was engrossed in the task he had been given. It being Morello, an American, who gave him the task, it is fair to say tasked with. Rob does not think he likes this American way of turning nouns into verbs. Some days he is sure he does not like it and could be moved enough to say so. Given the right circumstances he would say something. He would point it out to whoever was doing it. Task, he would say, is not a verb. It is a noun. Even if it was only himself doing it in his head. He would point it out to himself. He would pull himself up over it. Bring himself to task, you might almost say. The word is in his head now. Task task task. It is everywhere in his head. Other days he quite likes it, the turning of nouns into verbs. On these days he will give in to it. He will look for ways to do it. He will say, Why should it be only Americans who do it? He will see the point of it. He will take pleasure in doing it. Pleasure. There. That is a typical example of the kind of noun he will delight in turning into a verb, for there will always be something arch and ironic in his attitude as he does it. So he will say, it pleasures me. Meaning simply that it gives him pleasure.

He might for example, in fact this is what he is doing now, a sentence such as this is actually forming itself in his head now, Being tasked with long-listing agencies pleasures me.

But it is that time and although he has no desire to go to the pub with the others he needs to get something and he needs to get out, away from the i Satelliti S200 and the IBM ThinkVision L170P flat panel monitor. He needs to clear his head, if only of the word task.

He takes the Di Beradino classic. It is not that he needs it, he does not need it, he does not need what it contains. It is just that he has forgotten he does not need it. As soon as he is out of the building, as soon as he gets through the revolving door, he remembers that he does not need it. He thinks about taking it back to his workstation, that is how little he needs it. But he thinks it doesn't matter if he has it or he doesn't have it. So he will have it.

He will have the feel of the vegetable tanned leather in his hand. He will squeeze the stubby seam between his fingers. He will weigh its freight. He will feel its pull in his arm. He will think about the Snoopy ring binder and the Benjys napkin. But not in a needy way. There is something calmer about the way he holds on to these things today.

He has the letter to Emily Green in there now, on letterhead paper, Conqueror Smooth in Diamond White with the Diamond Life letterhead, inside a Conqueror Smooth Diamond White DL envelope. He has it in a different compartment, like it is on the other side of a balance. They are negative, it is positive. They balance each other out. The letter is to make up for the other things. He is looking for redemption from the letter. But he has not sent it yet. He has to find it in himself to send the letter to get the redemption. There is no stamp on the envelope.

He is thinking about food. He didn't realise he was so hungry until now. That is a good sign, he thinks. He is thinking about Pret. He thinks perhaps he will not go to Pret today. There are other places he can get a sandwich. He has read the comb-bound *Welcome to Diamond Life* document. It mentions numerous places you can get a sandwich, numerous is the word it uses. He is a marketing man. He will pick up on the word numerous. Part of his job is to comment on copy. He has read the brand guidelines. He believes himself to have a firm grasp of the brand tone of voice. He does not believe numerous is a word they should be using. Not even in an internal comb-bound document. It is about the brand. He should say something maybe but he won't. You have to know which ones are the ones you let go. Not on my watch comes into it as well.

He will try somewhere else. He will wander a little and find somewhere else to try. An independent sandwich bar. Those places make the best coffee, if they are run by Italians. He is not tied to Pret. He will have them make him up a customised sandwich. He does not need Pret. Yesterday was different. Yesterday he was vulnerable.

What about turning nouns into verbs that you then turn back into nouns, verbal nouns so to speak? These then replace the original nouns. He is thinking of the tasking. He is thinking of something like, I am tasked with long-listing agencies. The tasking pleasures me.

He will not go to Pret. He will look about him. He will take in his new environs. He likes the word environs. He likes to have the word in his mind as he looks around and does the taking in. He is a marketing man.

Driving through at weekends, he finds the City ominous. Without people, the high buildings crowd in on themselves over narrow streets. Driving through the City at weekends makes him think of neutron bombs. But with people, on a weekday lunchtime, there is not this feeling, or it is there only as an echo. The buildings need the people to make sense of them, the flow of people, the press of people, the weave the pulse the congregation. In a crowd it is possible to look into the eyes of a stranger. A man or a woman. It is possible to examine the faces of strangers, to look there for hope, to take hope from them. But the high buildings make him nervous even with this thronging in their shadows, this populating. High buildings have always made him nervous, especially unfinished or under repair buildings. There is this fantasy he has. He would date the onset of it to some time after his first sexual experience, perhaps immediately after, and it goes something like this: he imagines a girder falling from a high building and smashing through his skull and killing him. It can be a girder or a brick or a roof tile or anything construction related that is heavy and hard and high enough for its fall to kill him. There will be pain and blood and he will die. He does not have to be near a high building, whether unfinished or under repair or whatever, to indulge in this fantasy. He can be anywhere. But if he ever is in such a proximity, it is sure to flash through his mind, the fantasy of the falling girder. And he is sure now, able now, these days, being so long after his first sexual experience, to dispel it. All that is required is a conscious act of will on his part. He is able to give such a fantasy short shrift these days. Shrift is a word that is never used unless accompanied by short. One does not hear of long shrift for example. He is a marketing man. The point is he acknowledges the fantasy and then promptly dismisses it. It annoys him more than anything. It annoys him the way his brain keeps returning to this banal death wish as if for consolation. Does it console him? He thinks perhaps it does and the nervousness he claims is in fact a sham. Or can he be nervous and consoled at the same time? He thinks perhaps he can. He thinks perhaps he is.

He thinks there is something about imagining this thing happening that will prevent it from happening. He is nervous walking near tall buildings, especially those unfinished or under repair. He is also, and he being a marketing man he gropes for the right word, and the word that comes to mind is insured. This fantasy is his insurance policy. His nervousness is not a sham after all, it is his protection. His fear is what keeps him safe.

He does not look up at the buildings for confirmation of this idea. He looks into the eyes of strangers.

The first eyes that meet his are the eyes of a crash-helmeted man in a pale blue pilot shirt and dark polyester trousers. They are the kind of trousers that lose their shape at the knees and shine. The man is some way ahead of him, coming out of the HSBC bank. The man is carrying a moulded container, a security box, to which he is handcuffed. The box has the Securicor logo printed on the side. The same logo is stitched on the breast of the man's shirt. It is not on the helmet. You might expect it to be on the helmet but it isn't. Rob, certainly, as a marketing man, expects to see it on the helmet. He looks for the van. He looks for the logo on the van. The guard has just come out of the HSBC bank. The van should be just outside the HSBC bank but it is some way down the street. The van with the Securicor logo. It is closer to Rob. The guard with the Securicor security box in his hand is walking straight towards Rob. It seems that he has some business with Rob, that he is walking to Rob to hand him the Securicor security box maybe, so fixed is his gaze on Rob. But no. It is a coincidence. He is walking towards Rob because this is also towards the van. His gaze is fixed on Rob because it has to be fixed somewhere. It has to be fixed ahead of him. Rob is ahead of him. These eyes, that remind him of the grey forbo of his Unifor Progetto 25 screen facia, these eyes are possibly the least propitious eyes that Rob could look into. But the thing is they confirm his idea, the idea that fear is what keeps you safe. Here are eyes that are more fearful than his own. The man is paunchy, harassed and he has that pale, underpaid look. He has a bad diet. He eats Ginster pies, you imagine. You imagine if he takes his helmet off, which he is not going to do, but when he does, when he gets back to whatever place it is he feels safe enough to remove the helmet, you imagine his hair is thinning. And then there are the trousers that have lost their shape at the knees and are running to shine. But what money could be enough to undertake the holding of that moulded security box?

But at least he gets to wear a helmet, thinks Rob.

But it is not enough, of course. Nothing could be enough. He can tell that by looking into the man's eyes.

Something else he can tell from the Securicor security guard's eyes. Some reading of the street. The man is not looking at Rob now. He is reading the street and he has seen something and it is in his eyes. His eyes are big with it. And Rob has seen it, a part of Rob has seen it, though it is impossible. It is an impossible thing to have seen.

It is a gun, a handgun. It is a gun in the hand of a man who a moment ago was standing right in front of Rob, so close he could have touched him. That's how close he is to this man, to this man's gun, to the gun. He has never been this close to a gun before. He has never seen a gun. Not in broad daylight. Not ever. A gun is not something he sees. Not in the hands of the man right in front of him, the man so close he can touch him. He feels alive as he has never felt alive before. It strikes him as a miracle, this seeing of the gun. He is scared but he is alive. He thinks he is going to die. But he is alive. He thinks the gun will go off and the bullet will find him and he will die. But he is alive. He thinks it is not a man he is standing close to, not a man with a gun in his hand. He thinks it is his death. But he is alive. He thinks his own personal death has appeared before him as a man with a gun in his hand. And it is like a drug this being alive, it hits him like the effect of a powerful recreational drug. It is like an amphetamine-rush, a cocaine-jag, it is like a Viagra hard-on. It is a miracle. Because he knows that it is about to be taken from him. It is a miracle. And the gun is part of it, the gun is part of the miracle, the most important part.

He's dressed like he's in a film, Rob thinks. He's dressed like a man who holds a gun in a film would dress. It's not just the shades, the man is wearing shades and the blackness of the shades is impenetrable. It is a brand, Police maybe, or Ray-Ban, there is not time to be sure. Or DKNY. But the wearing of the shades is one thing and another is the suit, the man is wearing a suit. A sharp suit, a fashionable suit. Nice cut. He is smartly dressed. He had some idea of how you should dress to do this thing, to hold a gun in broad daylight on a busy street, and he has dressed himself accordingly. He wants to look the part. Boss. Paul Smith. Perhaps even it is a tailored suit. Who knows? The smartly dressed man with the gun in his hand is shouting. There is shouting. It is as if the smartly dressed man feels there should be shouting too. But also there is the sense that he cannot help himself. That as soon as you put a gun in your hand you will shout. He, the smartly dressed man, rushes the security guard with his shoulder down, while all the time shouting. All this happens quickly. In the same moment. The moment following the moment when the security guard's eyes read the street and see that he is there. The security guard sees the smartly dressed man. The smartly dressed man rushes the security guard. And there is the gun. And there is the fear in the security guard's eyes but it does not keep him safe. The shoulder of the smartly dressed man, his legs too, he does something with his legs, he knocks the security guard back and somewhat off balance though he does not fall to the ground. It seems that the security guard has it in his head that the one thing he must not do is fall to the ground. And all the time the smartly dressed man is shouting at him, like they are brawling in a pub. And there is the gun. Don't forget the gun. The impossible thing in the hand of the smartly dressed man. The gun. He is alive. It is out of control, neither of them can control it. The impossible thing in the smartly dressed man's hand flashes into the face of the security guard. Is this what they call pistol-whipping? Rob wonders. He has never been this close to a pistol-whipping in his life. His is not a life in which people get pistol-whipped, if this is indeed what pistol-whipping is. He is a marketing man. He is alive. Whatever you call it, there is blood in the security guard's face. Whatever you call it, the security guard is on the ground now, the force of it, the force of the pistol-whipping has finally knocked him off his feet.

The barrel of the gun, he has never had recourse to use that phrase, not in a real sense, not in a sense that pertains to something that has happened, is happening, in his own life. The barrel of the gun is in the security guard's face. The smartly dressed man is using the barrel of the gun to point to the blood in the security guard's face.

There is choreography to their movements. There is shouting. Give me the fucking case.

At Securicor we believe that security does not come in boxes but from the intelligent integration of products and services into a single service bundle.

The security guard does not fuck around. You would not fuck around. Rob does not fuck around. Not that there is any fucking around open to Rob, but he does not even think of fucking around. He does not look for a window in which to fuck around. He is not moving at all. He cannot move. His legs will not let him even if he wanted to. He does not want to. He thinks maybe the smartly dressed man is going to kill the security guard. He thinks maybe he should do something to prevent this. But he cannot see a way of helping the security guard without moving his legs and his legs will not move. And anyhow and anyhow and anyhow. He is alive. He is a coward and he is alive. He thinks maybe the thing to do is keep it that way. To remain a coward. To remain alive. To stay exactly where he is, not moving his legs, or any part of him. The smartly dressed man is bending over the security guard. Now would be a good time to do something. To make a move. To jump him. It would not take much to knock him off his balance. He is the closest to them. It would be embarrassing if someone else did something. But no one is doing anything. No one is moving.

The security guard has a key. He releases the handcuffs. He does not fuck around. Rob thinks he is right not to fuck around. He approves of the not fucking around. The smartly dressed man grabs the Securicor security box. It is his. He has it. He seems surprised by this. It is almost as if he does not want it now that he has it, as if he suspects it is a bomb that will go off in his hands. The point is he hesitates. Momentarily. Before running out into the road.

He has the Securicor security box in one hand, the gun, the impossible thing, in the other. People get out of the way. Cars swerve. He runs diagonally across the road, the gun held high, very much in evidence. This is the moment someone could get shot. Rob wonders what it's like to get shot.

There is a child, about seven, and her mother. The little girl is wearing the current little girl colour of the moment, lilac. Lilac pedal-pushers, lilac T-shirt. The T-shirt has a motif of heart-rending innocence. Groovy Chick, it says, below a picture of the Groovy Chick character. She has little girl eyes and little girl hair done in little girl bunches. What the fuck are they doing here? thinks Rob. That child should be at school, thinks Rob. They are standing on the other side of the road, at a Pelican crossing, waiting to cross, or maybe not, maybe they are just transfixed. The little girl eyes are looking at the impossible thing, the gun in the hand of the smartly dressed man.

The smartly dressed man is running straight for them. The girl does not know what to do about this man running straight into her. She doesn't know what to do about the gun in his hand. She doesn't know to get out of his way. That is too much to expect of a child. Rob is very scared. But he is alive. He thinks a man who is capable of holding a gun in broad daylight in a busy street is capable of shooting a child. He thinks so much that the smartly dressed man is going to shoot the little girl that he wonders if in some part of him he wants him to. That if the child is shot he will not be. He is a coward and he is alive. He thinks that the lilac and the Groovy Chick and the bunches will not save the girl. But there is no guarantee. Once the smartly dressed man starts shooting there is no saying where it will stop. The smartly dressed man runs into the child. In the end this is all that happens. The man runs into the child. The child falls over. The mother screams. The smartly dressed man shouts. Get out of the fucking way. He is not going to shoot anyone. He has what he wants. He has the Securicor security box and he has his shades and he has his suit. This is what he wants. He is running between pedestrians along the street. He has his gun in his hand.

Rob thinks now he can do something. Now he can move. The smartly dressed man is not going to shoot him now. He has his mobile. He should call the police. He even goes so far as to take the mobile out. The Sony Ericsson T610. He sees that he is not alone. All around him people are taking out their mobiles. Sony Ericssons, Nokias, Motorolas, Samsungs, NECs, Sagems, LGs, Alcatels. But above all Sony Ericssons. One woman is already talking into her phone. Yes. He's armed. He has a gun.

Rob looks up at the buildings, above street level. There are people at every window. Some are talking on phones.

He slips his mobile back into his jacket pocket.

The smartly dressed man runs into a side street. There is a second smartly dressed man revving a motorbike just around the corner. He too is wearing shades. The first smartly dressed man, the one with the Securicor security box and the gun, gets on behind him. Oh this is the moment he has been waiting for, you feel. There is something about the way he possesses this moment that you almost envy. Look at me, he is saying, not in words, but in the way he sits up and in the way he holds the gun. You could put me in a film, he is saying. This is what it would look like and this is how it would sound. The motorbike rumbles and roars. They do not wear crash helmets. Crash helmets would get in the way of the being looked at. Crash helmets would not look like in a film. If you have just done what they have just done you do not worry about the legal aspect. You do not worry about the safety aspect. If you have done what they have just done you know you are invulnerable. Look at me, the motorbike says in its rumble and roar. Everyone looks at the motorbike and the men on it. The motorbike overcomes its own indolence and speeds away with a slight wobble at the last.

30. The generic handkerchief

The Securicor security guard is on his feet now. He has blood in his face. It's streaming from his nose and he's blowing hard to keep from swallowing it. Rob takes out his handkerchief. It's a generic handkerchief but it's clean. He hands it to the security guard.

Here. It's clean.

The security guard seems confused by the handkerchief but he takes it. He is probably in a state of mind whereby he would be confused by anything and would take anything.

You've got blood, Rob explains, gesturing around his nose, a flat palmed hand making little circles over his nose.

The security guard nods. He appreciates the handkerchief. He appreciates the words. He wants to explain something.

We're told not to fight them. Hand it over. That's what we're told.

The Securicor security guard nods to the Securicor van, to the driver sitting behind the wheel.

He's not even allowed to get out of the van, explains the security guard.

Rob says, I can't believe they did it in broad daylight. In front of so many people.

They don't care. They don't give a shit.

The security guard wipes his face with the generic handkerchief. Rob can see his hand is shaking as he does it.

Are you all right? asks Rob. He knows it is a stupid question but he feels it has to be asked.

There's an ambulance on its way, someone says. It is the woman who Rob saw talking on the mobile. There is something peremptory in her tone that he does not like. He takes it as a criticism aimed at him but there is no reason. It is more likely that she is scared and this is how she sounds when she is scared. But she doesn't sound scared, she sounds impatient and angry.

The siren of a police car is suddenly with them. And the car. Two police officers get out. They are wearing bullet proof vests.

They are reassuringly big men. The bigness of the police officers reassures because you think they are not men who would fall over easily.

Which way they go?

The woman who sounds impatient and angry says, He ran into that street there. He had a friend waiting for him on a motorbike. He had a gun. Did they tell you he had a gun?

Neither of the police officers answers her question. They are too busy to answer questions. One is talking on his walkie-talkie, communicating the gist of what she has just said, through the mediation of police vocabulary. The word suspects is bandied about. The other is narrowing his eyes as he looks around, though he is probably doing something more technical than just narrowing his eyes and looking around.

And they have questions of their own.

Did you see the registration of the bike? asks the one on the walkie-talkie.

The woman's tone changes. She did not see the registration of the bike. She seems defeated by this.

The walkie-talkie police officer gets back in the car. He is so big it seems improbable that he will be able to. But he does. The hooping siren cuts in with a shattering blare. The police car jerks out like the walkie-talkie police officer has only just learnt to drive, not even passed his test, he doesn't even look.

The looking around police officer asks Rob, Did you see them?

Yes.

Were they black? White?

Rob is thrown by the question. They were very smartly dressed, he says. Like they'd seen a film and thought this was how you were supposed to dress to do a robbery.

You can't remember whether they were black or white?

Something in between, I think, he is forced to admit.

The woman has got her tone back. They were black, she says, rejoicing in her anger and impatience.

I didn't really focus on their colour, Rob says, making a point but feeling stupid.

The ambulance arrives, followed by more police cars. The police cars do not stop but follow the first up the side street to give chase.

The Securicor security guard holds the generic handkerchief out to Rob.

I'm sorry, he says. It's got blood on it.

That's all right, says Rob as he takes the generic handkerchief with the Securicor blood on. He tries to make the taking unhurried, calm. Insignificant. Yet his heart.

The looking around police officer is interviewing the woman with the tone. He looks up to see Rob take the generic handkerchief with the Securicor blood. He sees him put the handkerchief in his trouser pocket.

If you need me to be a witness, says Rob, aware that part of his reason for saying this is to distract the police officer from what he has seen.

Were you one of the ones who called us?

I was going to, but…

It's OK. We've got plenty of witnesses already.

Rob takes out a business card which he gives to the police officer. It seems strange giving a business card to a policeman. Especially a big one in a bullet proof vest.

Well, here's my card, anyhow.

The looking around police officer takes the card and puts it carelessly in a back pocket. He goes back to interviewing the woman with the tone.

Rob watches two green paramedics help the security guard into the ambulance. He starts to back away. It is over. He turns his back on it and walks away in earnest. A little way off, he stops and looks back. The green paramedics are closing the ambulance doors.

Rob takes out the generic handkerchief with the Securicor blood. He opens the Di Beradino classic and transfers the handkerchief inside.

31. The 5 Star Document Wallet

She's on her way to Compliance. She's holding a pink 5 Star Document Wallet with the new Guaranteed Bond brochure copy inside. She could email the copy but she welcomes the opportunity to get up from her desk and she thinks it's important to present these things in person. There are always fewer comments if you present the copy in person. She knows it should be fewer not less, she works in marketing. Sometimes she says less when she knows it should be fewer and even takes pleasure from it. She acknowledges a streak of perversity in her nature.

- *Made from 250gsm manilla*

She knows there will be comments. She is prepared for comments. She prefers to get them to read a hard copy and mark their comments on the hard copy. It's too easy if you email it. Email it as an attachment and they open it up and start rewriting it. This way there is no temptation for them to rewrite. She has spent too much time on Guaranteed Bond to have Compliance rewrite it. It is not their job to rewrite it. But she is prepared.

- *Half flap wallet*

She appreciates the walk. She appreciates the opportunity to look down from the gallery at the tree in reception. She waves to Donna. She is one of the ones who waves to Donna.

He is coming the other way. He has that briefcase. Whenever she sees him he always has that bloody briefcase. It is a nice briefcase but. Obviously he thinks someone is going to nick it. Obviously he thinks they are all thieves.

He's walking like a drunk at chucking out time. He must have been to the Feathers with the rest of them. He lurches from side to side. He's not used to it. Maybe they did it deliberately. They don't like him, she can tell. Ian and Geoff don't like him. Tony too, maybe. She's not sure. Tony is in a difficult position. Tony hired him. He has to work out otherwise Tony looks stupid. Tony is not stupid. It's in Tony's interest to help the guy. To make sure he settles in. To be nice to him. But he knows enough to feel threatened by this one. He hired him but. He is not stupid but. He wants him to work out but. There is always a but with Tony. The answer for Tony would be to do something like this. Take him out at lunchtime and get him drunk. It is his way of getting revenge. She has heard about the long list business. She has heard about the pitch. And also he would want to get back at him for the feeling threatened. She does not blame him. She understands. But she feels protective towards the new one.

She feels her hand grow damp where she's holding the 5 Star Document Folder.

- *Manilla used comes from sustainable forests*

He bumps into the wall. He is in a bad way. But he is not drunk, she realises. His face is grey.

She stops in front of him. She changes hands on the 5 Star Document Folder. She can feel it is losing its crispness at the point she has been holding it.

- *Assorted consists of pink, yellow, blue, green and red Size: Foolscap*

What now? she asks. She has to ask.

He shakes his head.

Tell me.

I just witnessed an armed robbery. He lifts his eyes. She remembers their different colours, the dappled apple effect of them.

Oh, yeah, I heard about that. She forgets his distress, is only excited. Everyone has been talking about the hold-up outside the HSBC.

They had guns. Guns. They were this close. As close as you are now. There is something pleading in his voice and in his eyes too. She doesn't like it.

But they didn't shoot you.

No.

She feels herself smile. She is surprised how easy it is after all. He is funny. There is something funny and touching about the way he said no. As if he is disappointed, as if it is humiliating for him not to be shot.

The guard was pretty badly shaken up, he insists.

She knows exactly what to say: But you're not him. Sorry. But it's right. You have to be glad that it wasn't you.

I don't know. It seems too harsh.

You can't go around suffering for every bad thing that happens in the world.

I'm not. It's just. A lot of bad things seem to be happening around me recently, he says.

She is starting to get angry. Is it anger? She feels something like anger. She feels goaded. It's the pleading tone. She does not want him to be a weak and pathetic man. She expects more of him than that. She puts him straight: Two. Two bad things.

In two days. And there have been other things. Not so major. But other things. I saw this girl get dumped.

Oh come on. She's already over it. You certainly should be.

He looks at her as if for the first time. He smiles. He stands up. He has been leaning against the wall but he stands up now. Yeah. OK. Thanks, he says.

Any time.

She tries to make it clear exactly what she means by this but finds she has lost the gift of smiling. She watches him head towards Marketing. There is a different quality to his unsteadiness. He is no longer in pieces. He is pulling himself together. He will be all right.

The 5 Star Document Folder is growing softer in her other hand now.

32. The Tracy Island movie tie-in toy

He's on the tube heading home. It's hot and crowded. By some fluke he has a seat. He feels guilty having a seat. He regrets taking it when it became available. It seemed the easiest thing at the time. It seemed perverse not to take the seat but now he has the seat he feels selfish and guilty. He does not want to be thought of as a selfish man, even by strangers.

The Di Beradino classic is on his lap. He opens it and looks in. The vegetable tanned leather smell. The Snoopy ring binder. The Benjys napkin. The generic handkerchief with the Securicor blood. His current paperback. The banana. He has forgotten to eat the banana. It annoys him when he forgets to eat the banana. The letter to Emily Green. Conqueror Smooth Diamond White. He takes out his current paperback and puts the briefcase on the floor between his feet. Since the lunchtime proximity of death his need for the Di Beradino has reasserted itself. He squeezes it between his legs, feels it with his ankles.

He tries to read but it's hard to concentrate.

He looks up. In the middle section of the compartment, where the double doors are, a child of no more than three is slung over his father's shoulder looking straight at Rob. It is disconcerting to find himself so regarded by a child. It seems to be, he has the sense, it is fanciful he knows, but he can't help feeling, it is not a little boy looking at him it is something else. The world. The universe. God. He does not believe in God, he certainly would not capitalise God. But. Here is this child looking at him like it means something. It is the randomness of it that makes it feel like it means something.

The kid is holding a piece of plastic crap, one of those giveaway toys you get with children's meals at McDonald's or Burger King or KFC. Some movie tie-in. You would say movie because it has to be movie if you are putting it next to tie-in. He is a marketing man. He cannot tell what film. He is not up on kids' films. It is not Shrek is all he knows. There is no professional reason for him to be up on kids' films. It is not easy even to tell what this toy is supposed to be. It is a piece of moulded ugliness. It does not have a face. It does not have wings. It does not have wheels. It does not have any recognisable form. It is brown and greyish green.

Whatever it is, the little boy drops it. He's too young to know that when you let go of something you lose it, which is anyhow a lesson it takes some people a lifetime to learn. The plastic clatter of its fall does not encourage hope. He starts wailing. And he's looking Rob in the eye all the time he's wailing as if he's conBarryd it's Rob's fault.

The father doesn't know he's dropped the toy. He's looking the other way. He might have heard the clatter or he might be one of those people who don't hear anything except what's going on in their own heads. Rob cannot tell anything about the father because he is looking the other way.

But the father hears the wailing. He pats his son on the head and speaks to him, though it's like an announcement for the rest of the compartment.

It's all right. We're nearly there. Not long now, I promise. I know, you're hot. I know. It's all right. Do you want a drink?

He starts to crouch down with the wailing kid on his shoulder. How hard it is, Rob thinks, to do anything when you have a wailing kid on your shoulder. He tries to imagine what the weight of the boy must be. What the strain must be it places on your shoulder and your back.

The man sinks to a half crouch and fishes around in a bag on the floor. But he doesn't know what's really upsetting his child. He doesn't know about the movie tie-in toy.

Rob doesn't know he's going to do it until he's doing it. There have been moments like this recently, moments in which he finds himself surprising. He gets up. He puts his current paperback in the Di Beradino as he gets up. He works his way through the straphangers, though there are no straps any more, there is a bar. He squeezes past the men pulling their shirts from their backs, suit jackets folded under their arms, past the women, past their bare waists, if there are bare waists, but there are armpits certainly, there are places where sleeveless cotton blouses cut away to reveal the concave complexity at the meeting point of arm and torso. And even that, in a stranger, seems too intimate a thing to brush against.

But he gets there. He does not falter. He does not back down. He goes through with it. He reaches the wailing child, who by now has refused the plastic bottle offered by his father. He gets there, Rob gets there, and he stoops and retrieves the movie tie-in merchandising toy and is able to examine it closely and he sees that it is some sort of geographical feature, an island, possibly, or a mountain. The boy has not taken his eyes off Rob the whole time it took him to get there. Nor has he stopped wailing. You would have thought the novelty of this man moving towards him would distract him from his grief, if only for a moment. Rob has the thing in his hand, he's turning it in his hand, examining it from every angle. And he doesn't know what he's going to do with it. He can give it to the kid or he can put it in the Di Beradino. He does not feel he can be seen whatever he decides to do. Everyone is invisible in crowded tube compartments.

He stands up and gives the toy back to the child. The little boy takes it but doesn't stop wailing.

The father has not seen any of this.

I know. You're hot. I'm hot. We're all hot.

Rob touches the man on his shoulder, the shoulder that doesn't have a wailing kid slung over it. The man is indeed hot.

There's a seat there, if you want it, says Rob nodding back to the seat he came from, relieved that none of the straphangers, though there are no straps, has taken it.

Thank you, says the father. He half crouches to retrieve his bag, then makes his way to the seat.

A woman, an older woman, about fifty or so, has seen all this and is beaming at Rob. He feels that he does not deserve her beaming. He feels that he has acquired her beaming under false pretences. She does not know that he has taken the Snoopy ring binder dropped by a Japanese student as she committed suicide. That he has a napkin with the tears of a dumped girl in a motif T-shirt. That he has the blood of an assaulted security guard. She does not know that he took these things deliberately. She does not know that he thought about taking the movie tie-in merchandising toy dropped by the wailing kid. That he came this close to putting it in his Di Beradino classic along with all the other mementos. There is no other word for them. They are mementos. He has not thought of calling them mementos before but this is what they are.

The woman is still beaming at him. They're inconsolable when they're that age, she says.

It's Tracy Island, he says. He makes it sound like an explanation. She doesn't understand his joke but he feels better for making it. And the thing is Rob hadn't known it was Tracy Island till he felt the words vibrating in his throat.

33. The Jonelle Egyptian Bath Sheet

Tonight he sounds like himself. The sound of his feet on the stairs is familiar and reassuring. He is taking the stairs at a run, two at a time. She can tell he is himself again.

She hears the inside door and waits. She waits and he doesn't come in. It's past the moment when he should be in the living room with her and she's anxious again.

She goes to see.

He's there in their pokey hall bending over his briefcase, moving things around in it. But he has his back to her so she can't get a good look at what he has there. There is something secretive in this shielding.

It is you. I thought I heard the door.

And there's something secretive in the way he closes up the briefcase hurriedly.

OK. Just, uh, checking something.

He stands up and turns to her. But his eyes do not look for hers.

I thought we could eat out tonight, she says. I haven't done anything.

I just need to get out of these clothes. He's taking his jacket off as he moves into the bedroom. I think I might just have a quick shower, he calls back to her.

He comes out of the bedroom without his jacket. He pulls his shirt away from his armpits.

Sticky, he tells her.

Urggh! Go on then. Hurry up, hurry up.

You don't have to talk to me like I'm one of your bloody brats.

She decides to take it as a joke. Yes I bloody do. Hurry up, Saunders, or you won't get any dinner, she says, trying to slap him on the rear as he passes on his way to the bathroom.

He does not respond.

No horrible meetings today? she calls into the bathroom, repentant.

There's a pause. He's thinking about it? At last he calls, No.

That's good.

He comes back out, his shirt undone.

Actually quite a good meeting. We're going to put the business up for review. Morello asked me to oversee it. Well, the initial stages anyhow.

He manages to keep the enthusiasm out of his voice.

That's great. That's really great. Who's Morello?

The C.E.O.. The big cheese.

Oh, good.

She nods for him to go back into the bathroom.

Shower, she says, risking his annoyance. I'll get you a clean towel. This is her peace offering.

While he is showering, she takes a big white towel from the airing cupboard in the hall. She sees the Jonelle label, 100% Egyptian cotton. She touches the towel to her face, comforted by its warmth. She loves the smell of clean towels. She does not use fabric conditioner. It is just the smell of towels she loves.

Jonelle towels made from 100% Egyptian cotton, with more, longer loops than the average towel, giving maximum absorbency, softness and durability. Made in England. Machine washable at 60°C.

She is not wholly resistant to the charms of fabric conditioner. Her mother is a great one for fabric conditioner, always has been. She grew up clothed in the fragrance of Lenor. That was the smell that greeted her as she opened her drawers. But now the smell of cleanliness is enough for her. The smell of cleanliness, which is the lack of the smell of everything else, of sweat, of germs, of blood, of come, of skin molecules rotting, it is the smell of cleanliness that is essential to her. She recognises the fraudulence of fabric conditioner. It has a manufactured fragrance. She can see the attraction, she can imagine falling for it, in a moment of weakness maybe. She has in the past. Comfort, there is even a brand called Comfort, though they were always a Lenor family. But she made a decision, at some point she must have made a decision. To eschew fabric conditioner. She thinks it was a conscious decision, though not a momentous one.

Does it have something to do with her relationship with her mother? she wonders. Is it one of the ways she has chosen to mark herself out as an individual distinct from her mother? Is it even an act of rebellion?

The thing is, the towel's cleanliness, this Jonelle Egyptian Bath Sheet's cleanliness in her hands now, its simple cleanliness, it is a thing of the moment and it is treasured for its impermanence. The fakery of fabric conditioner is that it seeks to prolong the moment of cleanliness and she feels instinctively that that is wrong. So it is all to do with mortality. Even the fabric conditioner turns out to be connected to death and time, the passage of time, the hurrying towards death. Whether it is something you accept, accepting and rejoicing in each moment you are given, such as the deep inhaling of a fresh but unconditioned towel. Or whether you go for fabric conditioner.

She read somewhere that fabric conditioner can be linked to cancer. It leeches chemicals into the skin, she read, which cause cancers. Perhaps her eschewing dated from the moment she took on that information or misinformation, she has never got to the bottom of it. So it is about fear in the end. Choosing one form of comfort over another.

So he is out of the shower now and she has to surrender the Jonelle Egyptian Bath Sheet and its impermanent cleanliness. It will begin its dampening now, its decay. And there is a sadness, a regret, a grief, associated with this loss, but as these things go they are minuscule emotions, only reminders of a greater grief.

Perhaps as she gets older she will start using fabric conditioner. Maybe that is what happens. It is something we use to mask the smell of our dying, she thinks.

By now he's changed into a pair of clean Dockers Icon Plant Seasonals in stone, with a black Muji V-neck T-shirt. The damp Jonelle Egyptian Bath Sheet is discarded. His freshly showered hair lies dark and slick. She wants to breathe in the scent of him. His cleanliness now has the same effect on her as the cleanliness of towels. But she's hungry too and wants to hurry him out of the door.

Shoes? she reminds him unnecessarily. He slips on his casual pair, Clarks Unify in dark and light taupe.

They are ready to go. She has the door open. At the last he picks up his briefcase. It seems he wants to take it with him.

What do you want that for?

It's got some, uh, confidential papers in it. To do with the pitch. I don't really want to leave it here, in case...

In case of what?

Burglary?

She laughs. In amazement. Oh, I see. You think we're going to get burgled tonight?

It's just a precaution. Maybe taking the briefcase will make sure we don't get burgled. You know, when you prepare for the worst, the worst doesn't happen.

You are a strange, strange person.

It's called insurance.

She smiles and shakes her head. He is serious about this, she can see. She is better placed than most to take this sort of thing in her stride. Her children. She is used to the strange attachments children form with things. She is familiar with the idea of the comfort blanket. And he wonders why she sometimes falls into talking to him like he is one of her children.

34. The Cobra Premium Beers

There is comfort in the cold cutting clarity of the Cobra Premium Beers.

The first sip is everything. The beer, the cold bottled beer, is never as cold or as welcome as in that first sip. It is the precise moment that anticipation and fulfilment collide. It does not come again. You only have one shot at the first sip.

There is silence between them. Rob feels the need to speak but he does not want to talk about his day. The last thing he wants to talk about is his day. There is a danger though that if he says nothing he will spend the evening fingering the condensation on his Cobra bottle. He does not want to do that. It will warm the beer.

He does not like the new bottles with the fancy embossed symbols. He considers them over-designed, over-marketed. He liked the old bottles. What was wrong with the old bottles? he wants to know.

They talk about the new bottles. Julia likes the new bottles. She does not see the virtues of the old bottles. He points out the virtues of the old bottles. The old bottles were more Indian, he maintains. The old bottles had simplicity and charm on their side.

Isn't that rather patronising? she wonders. Isn't it, couldn't it be accused of being, she pauses not sure if she can say the word, racist?

Not at all, he counters. It was a fake simplicity, a fake charm. The whole thing was very sophisticated. Very clever, in marketing terms, to appear so naïve as a brand.

The bottom line is he does not like the embossed symbols. There is too much the temptation to finger them. He is a great one for fingering beer bottles and he hates himself for it. And pulling off labels.

So how was your day? He asks the question, he's dreading it so much, he decides the thing to do is ask it first.

My day? Oh, you don't want to know.

Yes I do, he insists.

She smiles. She is happy. He is glad he insisted, though again there is that feeling that he doesn't deserve this. Her happiness.

OK, she says, putting herself into the telling. Well, I had a very unpleasant scene with Finlay Reardon's mother.

What about? He is concentrating on the embossed symbols. He cannot stop fingering them.

Well, you know we've been having this Music Week thing? She said she might be able to help out for one of the sessions. But I needed to know for definite yesterday. And she didn't drop Finlay off yesterday. It was the father for some reason. And he didn't know anything about it. So I had to ask one of the other mothers if she could do it. Well, Sheila Reardon turned up this morning with her violin, as if we'd definitely arranged it, which we hadn't. And when I told her that Tiffany Barker's mother was going to do something instead she flew off the handle. In front of the children as well.

He feels himself grimace. There is something artificial about the grimace, he feels.

I tell you, I'll be glad when it's half term, she says.

I'll drink to that.

Cobra Premium Beer. The extra smooth, less gassy premium beer.

There is silence between them. They watch the waiters.

I'm starving, says Julia.

Me too.

The popadoms arrive. They snap the popadoms delicately. It is a pact they have. They are never brutal with the popadoms.

How do you fancy going to Dorset this weekend? There is a tentative anxious quality to her voice. It matches the snapping of the popadoms.

I don't think I can. He is too quick to say this. He knows he is too quick. I mean, this review business. I may have to work.

The weekend?

I'll have to see.

I said we'd go. I said to Mum we'd go.

You can go. If I can I'll come. But. I'll have to see.

There is silence between them. He looks for meanings in the embossed symbols on his 660ml Cobra Premium Beer bottle. This is something you could not do with the old bottles, he thinks. He is warming to the new bottles.

35. The Eurocopter EC135 Advanced Police Helicopter

He feels like a god, or a guardian angel. He has the roar of thunder, he has the power of thunder. He has the cloak of invisibility. He is enclosed in a capsule of darkness. From the capsule, a searching beam, the beam of the Spectrolab Nitesun II searchlight. His all-seeing eye. He has the roar. His presence is felt. He knows that they will be looking up to see him now.

As helicopters go, the Eurocopter EC135 Advanced Police Helicopter is quiet. As helicopters go. Even so, he is sitting in the midst of the roar of thunder.

The voices in his helmet speak to him. They are like prayers, petitioning, beseeching, appeasing.

Roger that.

He knows that he inspires awe. That's the point. The point is to be seen, for the beam of the Spectrolab Nitesun II to be seen, and for the roar of the Eurocopter EC135 to be heard. Though he is invisible, the point is for them to know he is there.

He knows that he inspires fear.

He is repaying fear with fear.

He thinks of Ginny's fear and knows that he is right to be there. He is there for her. And for the boy.

Ginny complains to him about his job. She doesn't want him flying the Eurocopter EC135 Advanced Police Helicopter. Christ, she doesn't even want him in SO13. She's scared. You could get killed, she says. It's dangerous, she says.

These are all things he knows. She does not need to remind him.

Optimised for airborne surveillance, the EC135 Advanced Police Helicopter, provides a uniquely capable, low noise, low vibration surveillance platform. Equipped with suitable video-down link equipment supplied by McAlpine Helicopters Ltd, the Advanced Police Helicopter becomes the Police 'Eye-in-the-sky' ensuring the best co-ordination between the ground based officers and their air support. The APH is fitted with the McAlpine developed Police Mission Pod now offered as part of any McAlpine Helicopters Ltd EC135 public service completion.

You're a father now, she says.

His son Dean, twenty months into his life, a baby boy he can lay on his chest to sleep and the weight of him is no trouble, for hours he can have him there on his chest sleeping, as he inhales the blondness of his hair, admires the delicacy of his ears, wonders at the fine creamy perfection of his skin.

You're a father now, she says.

That's the point, he says. I'm doing this because I am a father. I can think of no better way to protect my son. It's for Dean that I'm doing this. For his heedless laughter and his innocent tears, to preserve his laughter and his tears, that's why I'm doing this, he thinks.

And if you get killed, how will that protect him?

But he will not get killed. He has the roar of thunder. He has the searching all-seeing eye, the beam of the Spectrolab Nitesun II searchlight. He is cloaked in dark invisibility. He has voices in his helmet. He has the Eurocopter EC135 Advanced Police Helicopter. It is impossible for him to be killed.

36. The Martyn Gerrard window

It's a clear night, warm. There is silence between them and a distance. She wants to hold him. Put her arm around him or hold hands, just to hold hands. She has wanted to do this since they left the Shamrat. She feels it will go some way to making amends. She has the sense that she needs to make amends but she's not sure what for.

If I have offended you, she thinks but doesn't say.

The thing is he has that bloody bag. The bag has become something between them.

She is thinking this and then she can think nothing more. Her thoughts are hammered out of her by a sudden shattering of the silence between them. A thrashing and savaging of the night. A churning of the distance between them.

They pause and look up to watch it. The helicopter is hovering in the mid-distance, a brilliant beam of light coming out of it, scanning the ground below.

It's police, he says.

What are they doing?

Looking for trouble.

Here?

It's not as close as it looks. Or sounds.

It sounds like it is in their heads.

It could be a mile away, he goes on. A mile east of here. The mosque. That's where the mosque is.

But what do they hope to see?

The helicopter suddenly flies off. It takes its clattering din with it and the shooting beam.

At last she puts her arm around him. It is a difficult thing to do but she has wanted to do it for so long. He is only a little taller than her but still she has to reach up. She feels his tenseness tighten.

You are behaving strangely at the moment. Admit it, she ventures.

Am I?

Yes.

It's my first week in a new job. Aren't I allowed to be tense? As long as that's all it is.

She drops her arm. It's too hard, too high. But still she craves proximity. She nestles her head against his shoulder. She's feeling for some relaxation on his part. Instead there is a further tensing. She gives up. That bloody bag. It's the bloody bag that's holding him away from her.

It's just, sometimes, you know. He must feel he owes her something. An explanation. She is a little angry now. He is right to pick up on that, if he has. But he's struggling with his explanation: I think, I can't help thinking… it's all a waste of time, isn't it?

What? She does not keep the anger from her voice. The fear too. Is he talking about them? Why does she feel he is talking about them?

What I do, he confesses.

Relief. That's all it is: what he does. A smile bubbles in the darkness. He's still talking, trying to give her the explanation she deserves.

Insurance, he says. Selling insurance. That's all I am, a glorified insurance salesman. And it doesn't actually help anyone, does it? It doesn't stop bad stuff happening. And that's what people really want.

Well, you can't, she says. She's not angry any more. She feels magnanimous. She is happy to be talking to him. She wants to help him. You can't stop bad stuff happening. But, I would think, having the right insurance, makes it less bad. You know, financially.

Yeah, but the reason people do it, the reason people pay their premiums year after year, is to stop shit happening. Really. Deep down. That's what they want. And all they're actually doing is throwing money away. Most people pay out far more in premiums than they ever claim back from an insurance company.

Well, yes. She is amused. She answers him forcefully and with amusement. Otherwise the insurance companies would go bust, she says.

Yeah, I know. His tone suggests an admission. He's admitting his absurdity. He's sharing in her amusement. She feels she's turned it around.

They are standing in front of an estate agent's window, in front of the Martyn Gerrard window.

How did we get here? she laughs. She knows that she has steered him. She wanted to show him this, these properties for sale. Subconsciously perhaps. She will blame her subconscious, but she knew she was bringing him here.

It is something from time to time they like to do, to look in estate agents' windows. She will read out the details to him, well presented flat offering a good deal of space, in a leafy residential area, stripped wooden floor, duplex flat, own rear garden, the property benefits from a balcony, within easy reach of local amenities. And he will make his wry dry comments, translating the estate agent speak for her amusement, one up from pokey, there's a tree at the end of street, gaping floorboards, the floor in the hall slopes, you can keep the window box, right next door to the local crackhouse.

But tonight it doesn't feel right. She senses he doesn't want to play, she doesn't attempt it. They stand and read the cards in silence. Or she reads. She cannot be sure he even sees them.

But now his arm is around her. He pulls her to him finally. He allows the nestling of her head on his shoulder.

I'd love a house, she murmurs. He does not answer. Maybe he didn't hear. She hopes he didn't hear.

37. The Marvelon contraceptive pill

It is Tuesday. She pops the next TUE pill from the blue plastic dispenser trademarked Marvelon, forcing it through the foil top. The Marvelon trademark in stylised handwriting typeface has a vaguely retro feel, she thinks of it as fifties-ish. The typeface seeks to conjure up a pre-permissive innocence. It seeks to reassure. It seeks to say this is not about the hormones of your body. This is not about powerful chemicals. This is vaguely reminiscent of a Hannah-Barbera cartoon, it seeks to say. The Flintstones or the Jetsons. There is nothing scary about this, the Marvelon trademark typeface seeks to say.

She takes the Marvelon contraceptive pill, the tiny white weightless pill, and it feels like she is taking the sacrament. It is a consecrated pill on her tongue. This is blasphemy, she knows. She was confirmed. The blasphemy shocks her. Body of Christ. To think of the body of Christ at this moment, the moment she is taking the Marvelon contraceptive pill. Nothing could be further from the body of Christ, she thinks, nothing could be further from the holy mother of God, from the son of God, from the virgin birth, than this unvirgin unbirth. It is the anti-sacrament, she thinks.

She is not religious but.

To think of the body of Christ at the moment she is taking the Marvelon contraceptive pill.

She is in bed, next to a man she is not married to, taking a pill that will allow them to have sex without creating life. She is confirmed. She received the sacrament in confirmation of her faith.

She is not Catholic but. High Church is her background. A long time ago now but it is always there with you.

She believes there is a god. She really does. She doesn't think about it much. She believes without thinking about it much. But it is a question, if you asked her, do you believe in God, she would say yes. If one of the children asked her, for instance. It has happened. Children want to know such things. Do you believe in God, miss? Yes. It has to be like that with children.

And here she is in bed next to a man she is not married to, preparing herself to have sex with him, thinking of the body of Christ at the moment she is taking the Marvelon contraceptive pill.

She is shocked and ashamed but there is something fake about her shock and her shame.

Really it is no big deal. Really she is not shocked at all or ashamed. She only thinks she ought to be.

She tries to get to the bottom of what it means.

To think of the body of Christ at the moment she is taking the Marvelon contraceptive pill.

She realises what it's all about is she hates the pill. Fundamentally, at a deep level, at a spiritual level, a religious level, she is not religious but, she hates the pill. The blasphemy was meant to shock her into realising this. She wants to come off the pill. It is more than just the pill is a nuisance. It is more than just she is worried about the long term health effects.

She hates the clever chemical trickery that's being perpetrated on her body. The suppression of ovulation. She realises she wants to ovulate. She does not, any longer, want to get in the way of ovulation.

She's popping out the days of her life, each pill a little closer to the end. The end of the dispenser. Onto the next dispenser. Pop the days. End of another dispenser. Onto the next. Pop the days. Until. Until the end of the last dispenser. Until the end.

Each pill is like a little death. She feels this now for the first time and it depresses her.

She puts the current Marvelon dispenser on the bedside table, next to the Philips AJ3120 radio alarm clock.

In 1998 cumulative sales of Marvelon and other oral contraceptives containing desogestrel exceeded one billion worldwide, confirming its acceptability and safety.

He's reading his current paperback. She wants to talk about what she's feeling. She feels it's important to tell him what she's feeling. She's not sure exactly what she's feeling but telling him will help her know.

Rob, she says, and her voice is fragile and fearful. She does not know how he will take it. She has no idea what to expect from him. It could mean the end, she realises. This could be the end of them.

Mmmm? He is distracted is not a good sign. She needs his full attention for this.

Please.

He puts the book down and turns to her. They kiss. That is to say his mouth seeks out and finds hers, their lips press into their lips. There is something electric, tangibly electric, the moisture, the heat, a jolt, something passes between the moisture and heat of their lips in the first touch. But it feels strange to be doing this, she cannot shake off the feeling of its strangeness. There was distance between them and silence between them. And she has this thing to tell him. This thing that could mean the end of them. She is serious about this. If she tells him this thing and he does not accept it, she cannot in all seriousness see how they can go on. It is an ultimatum. She realises she is about to give him an ultimatum. And this is not what she meant, this kissing. Her Please was not Please kiss me it was Please you must listen to this this is serious. Their lips are pressed into their lips. They are kissing. The kiss continues. This is not what she meant. This is not what she wanted. She has taken the Marvelon contraceptive pill but it is not now tonight her intention to have sex with him. They must talk before that can happen. She must tell him how she feels and he must accept it.

There must be nothing between them, no silence, no distance.

Now he's kissing her neck and shoulders and there's a danger that she might give in to this. The kissing on the mouth was not so dangerous. But this. She closes her eyes. She is smiling. She can almost forget her fears, her hatred for the little blue dispenser. The thing she has to tell him. Almost forgotten. But.

She opens her eyes. She pulls away.

Rob, she insists. She is gentle and considerate and fearful for him, for them both, but she insists.

Mmmm? He is bent forward, still trying to kiss her neck and shoulders, knowing this is something she loves. She is rolling her neck like a horse rolls its neck, half in pleasure, but half because she wants him to stop. She's beginning to feel the effect of the kissing all over, in her nipples particularly. He's kissing her neck and she's acutely aware of the sensitivity of her nipples.

She puts hands on him and pushes him away.

Please, she says. This is important.

He frowns.

I want to come off the pill. She wonders if she wants to punish him, if the abruptness of the announcement is designed to punish him.

You what?

I want to come off the pill. I've been on it since I was nineteen. I think it's time I came off it.

But what would we do?

Do?

About contraception?

Well. That's a good question. That's a very important question.

She hears herself and thinks, I sound like I'm talking to one of the children.

You're thinking condoms? There is a dead, heavy disappointment in his voice.

No, actually. She hesitates before taking the plunge. I was thinking nothing.

Nothing? What do you mean? Nothing.

I mean we don't use any contraceptive.

But… you could get pregnant. There is a laugh in his voice but he is not finding this funny.

That would be the idea.

No. No, no, no-no-no!

Well, that's fairly conclusive, she says. She feels a coldness spread through her. She is close to tearful. It is the end. Does he realise it is the end of them?

No, I didn't mean it like that. It's just, it's all so sudden.

It's not sudden to me. I've been living with this for years. It's with me always.

But you only just told me.

She realises he has a point. Maybe she is not being fair to him. Maybe she needs to give him time is all it is. But the blue plastic foil topped dispenser trademarked Marvelon does not give her time, it takes it away. Day by day, it takes her life away from her.

She relents. She will try to explain it to him. Try to help him understand. I'm three years older than you, remember, she says. I don't have forever. I can't put it off forever.

We can't possibly bring a child into this world, he says.

Don't give me that. That's bullshit. She's angry now.

I'm serious.

Is that really what you think?

Yes. I do. Seriously.

She shakes her head and turns her back on him. Throws herself heavily down onto the bed.

You watch the news, he says.

We don't get earthquakes in this country.

It's not just earthquakes.

It's an excuse.

Tonight. I was coming home on the tube. There was this little boy.

Other people's children are different.

You haven't heard what I was going to say.

She sits up and looks at him.

How do you protect them? From pain. From all the terrible things that could happen to them. I mean, this kid, he just dropped his toy, some worthless piece of junk, and you should have seen how he cried. I mean what if something really bad had happened to him?

Why should it? Why do you assume that something bad will happen?

Because.

I don't understand. It's not as if anything really bad has ever happened to you.

Maybe that makes it worse.

I don't see that it would. Why should it?

If the worst happens, and you survive it, you're stronger. Less afraid.

It's almost as if you're wishing for the worst to happen.

He says nothing. He lies back with his eyes open.

She throws herself back down on the bed, her back to him. She is looking at the blue plastic dispenser trademarked Marvelon, the hated fake retro typeface. It is the last thing she wants to look at but she cannot bring herself to look at him right now.

The light, she says.

He turns off the bedside light. It is down to him to turn off the bedside light.

38. **The Barbour Harris Tweed jacket**

He has on the orange Nike Air Zoom Elite running shoes. He's running. He runs from the day before. From the night. He runs into the new day. Each day is a separate universe. Yet there is the thing she said. It's still with him, the thing she said. He cannot run from the thing she said.

There's a dog barking. Its barking is insistent, the same noise repeated monotonously. It is a disturbed, angry pulse. It's disrupting his pace. He tries to match his pace to the animal pulse. It doesn't work. The barking is on a different cycle to his steps. It jars. He's thrown. His pace is shot.

And then suddenly there is a high-pitched yelp and the dog is silent.

He enters Queen's Wood. He runs up the bank, past the low wall at the entrance, his orange Nike Air Zoom Elites pounding the track.

The thing she said is still with him.

He follows the track. The track takes him between trees, alongside a ditch. He leaps the ditch. The track takes him down into the wood. The track takes him through the wood. He can lose the thing she said here in the wood.

He's not thinking about the thing she said anymore, he's thinking, It's usually about now that I see him. And he has in his mind an image of the spaniel, a Springer Spaniel he thinks it is, and the dog in his mind is eager and pleased to see him, as always. Maybe it was the barking that made him think of the dog.

He's thinking about the dog as the track takes him down and round. And there to one side, just off the track, he sees the dog but it is not eager and pleased. It's lying motionless on its side on the leaf-softened twig-scattered earth and there is blood, blood in its fur, blood in its fur around its head, and darkness that can only be blood on the earth. And it's not moving. The thing about this dog is that it is always moving, he has never seen it not moving, it runs, leaps, jumps, trots and springs, it is a Springer, it springs. But the dog is not moving. It doesn't make sense. This dog doesn't make sense if it isn't moving. There is blood in its fur, actually a dark mangled wound in its head, on the crown of its head between its ridiculous spaniel ears.

He slows to a halt with the dog at his feet. The loudest sound in the wood is his breathing.

He looks down at the unmoving dog. He can see that it is a bitch. He must accept that it is dead and yet it is hard for him to do this. Some part of him loves this dog. He is stricken by its death and he is scared. Something did that to it. Something killed it. Something loveless and hard and cruel.

He hears and sees at the same time, the hearing is definite, the seeing subliminal, but he does, he thinks he does see something move. Off to the right, the same side of the track as the dog is lying but farther off into the trees. It is some movement in the trees, a low branch stirring.

He calls out. It is a desire to create something louder than his breathing. It is a desire to show himself a man in the face of this. But he is scared. He feels himself watched by the wood. And by something in the wood.

Hello?

The wood swallows the word.

He looks down at the dog again.

A question he cannot form is building pressure in his head.

Hello? he calls again.

The wood is voracious for his words. They disappear without trace. He has the feeling, really he does, that the same will happen to him.

But he has to form the question. The pressure of it remaining unformed is too much for him. Where is the dog's owner, the man who never acknowledges him?

He steps over the Springer Spaniel.

He's off the track now. He's in amongst the trees. He's heading for the spot where he heard and possibly saw the movement. Not running, going as slow as it is possible for a man to go and still be moving. This is the locus of his fear. It is madness to approach it. The ground is crackling under his orange Nike Air Zoom Elite running shoes. Each poised and prolonged step crackles.

The first thing he sees are the feet. The feet loom up from the ground, the smooth soles of the shoes pointed towards him.

He'd like to keep looking at the shoes, the brown brogues with their smooth beige soles. But he can't. There is something else he must look at. The shoes are perfect. The shoes are immaculate. He could look at the shoes forever. But there is something else demanding his attention.

He tears his eyes away from the shoes. He looks at the face, he looks into the eyes, and sees that the glasses are askew on the face and that the eyes are open and staring straight at him but of course these eyes do not acknowledge him. He can see that there is something terribly wrong, that the man will never acknowledge him now, that the man has missed his chance for acknowledging forever. There is blood, there is a mangled bloody mess in his forehead, there is a breach in the surface of the head, a horrible bloody wound that is deep and gaping and rough and who could have done this and how. A brutal force, a brutal concentration of violence, of hatred, of rage has caused this glistening. And he has the temptation to put his finger into it and take something from it.

He looks about. Still that sense of being watched, though now he thinks it is not the woods watching him, nothing so fairytale as the trees watching him, how fanciful and naïve an idea that seems now. The movement that he saw, the watching that he feels, it is the perpetrator, he finds the word perpetrator somehow, when murderer will do.

The thing to do: to run off now, to scarper, that's the word, the precise word for what he must do. He is a marketing man. Scarper. He can run back to the flat and alert the police from there. Alert, yes. Leave it to the police. Let them sort it out. Let them deal with the perpetrator, murderer if you like, because this must be murder. There is intent in that wound, there is consideration in that bloody focus of hatred.

So that is what he must do. The thing he must not do is carry on looking at the wound, the last thing he should do is carry on looking for fragments of bone, tiny splinters of skull they are, amongst the dark pulpy mush of the brain. And the very last thing he must do is what he finds himself doing now.

He drops to a crouch over the body. This is madness, he thinks. Even he thinks this is madness.

But he must take something.

He has the man's jacket between the fingers of his hand, feeling the texture of the tweed and the smoothness of the lining. On one lapel he notices a small enamel badge. It is a simple black square with the letters NLHS in brass.

He unbuttons the jacket. It has come to this, unbuttoning the jacket of a dead man. He opens the jacket and sees the word BARBOUR on the label, beneath it Harris Tweed.

He can tell himself he is looking for ID. Though of course he is looking for something to take. It has come to this, it has come to a compulsion, but he remains wonderfully clear-sighted even in the grip of the compulsion, his compulsion, it is his. He realises this is something he will risk his life for, this taking. He feels the risk now, the danger is present and invigorating. He feels alive.

He sees a bulge in the lining. The pocket behind the BARBOUR Harris Tweed label bulges. His hand goes into the pocket behind the BARBOUR Harries Tweed label. He has thought about putting a finger into the bloody wound. He has played with the idea of putting a finger into the bloody wound and touching a splinter of bone and pulling his finger away with the splinter of bone on the end of his finger. He has thought about doing it. He will settle for this. His hand in the pocket behind the BARBOUR Harris Tweed label. Spiritually it is equivalent. He is going into the same place. He is going into the heart of his fear.

He takes it out, the thing that bulges, the man's wallet it is. He has its weight, its leather, is it leather or something trying to be leather, surface in his hands. It must be leather. The man's immaculate brogues persuade him that it is leather.

What he did not expect. He has the man's wallet open in his hands and he did not expect this, he was not looking for this, this is exploding in his heart, the unexpectedness of this. Money. The man's wallet is stuffed with notes. Fifties, they are all fifties. He thumbs the fifties. There must be, he cannot say, his mind has gone blank, he cannot count, there must be. Thousands, there must be thousands.

This is not what he wants. This is not what it has come to. Better to take a piece of bone from the bloody mess than to take this money. He closes the wallet and tries to return it. But he's fumbling, he fumbles it. He can't get the pocket open enough, he can't get the wallet in the pocket. It's harder to put the wallet back than take it out. It is as if the dead man is refusing to take it back, as if his Barbour Harris Tweed jacket is rejecting it.

Take the wallet, take the fucking wallet, the dead man is saying to him. That's what you want, the wallet, the money, that's what you want, isn't it?

He's sweating. His sweat drips onto the dead man. Why did he start this? What if someone comes? I'm looking for ID he would say. That will be his excuse.

Of course, the ID. But he doesn't want to look for ID. He wants to get the wallet back in the pocket and get away from there, away from his fear. To scarper.

He gets the wallet back in the pocket behind the BARBOUR Harris Tweed pocket. The bulge looks different, but who is to know? But the bulge looks incriminating. They will know from the bulge that someone has been in that pocket, that someone has had the wallet out. They will know from the bulge that it was him. They will know.

And there is the sense of being watched. Whoever is watching him will tell them. I may be the perpetrator, he will say, whoever is watching him will say, I may be the murderer, if you insist, but I saw him take the wallet out of the Barbour Harris Tweed jacket, out of the inside pocket of the Barbour Harris Tweed jacket.

Rob has the sense that he will be judged more harshly than the murderer, that his act will be considered more inexplicable and therefore beyond the pale.

So what he should do is run. He has not forgotten the importance of scarpering.

But he does not do it. He reaches to the lapel. He lifts the lapel. He unclips the pin of the badge. He has the badge, the black badge with the letters NLHS, he has it in the clench of his hand.

He rises and looks around one final time.

The thing she said, with bitterness he remembers the thing she said. He has a mind to bring her here and show her this. Let's talk of having children when you have seen this, he thinks. His hand clenches around the enamel badge. He turns and tiptoes away from the body, tiptoes out of the trees, back on to the track and runs.

39. The Sony KV-20FV10 20" WEGA TV

She's standing in front of the TV. It is the first generation of Sony Wegas, charcoal grey not silver. Only five years old but it looks dated now. Dark and a little boxy in comparison. Everything is silver now. He has taught her to notice such things though she cannot bring herself to care.

It was one of the first things they bought together, certainly their first major purchase. They got it from Dixons in Brent Cross. She's trying to count the years back, remembering when she moved in. Over five years ago now she moved in. The TV was bought soon after that. The TV is almost as old as their relationship. She can remember him taking it out of the box. She can remember his face, the contagious pleasure in his face. She would not describe herself as someone who is moved by material objects, but she was moved by his pleasure. It was he, after all, who had insisted on getting a Sony Wega. She can remember the polystyrene blocks. She can remember leaving the box and the polystyrene blocks for the binmen. She can remember her fear, that someone would see the box and the polystyrene blocks and put two and two together. Two and two together being they have a new TV, let's break in and nick it.

But she can remember too the feeling of newness and optimism, the excitement you would say, the feeling you get when you unpack a new TV. That is a feeling. It was there in his face.

Features:
*   *20-inch TV with Trinitron flat screen; 22.12 x 18.38 x 19.75 inches (W x H x D)*
*   *3-line digital comb filter improves image resolution and clarity*
*   *SpeedSurf rapid channel surfing, 5 favorite channel presets, and sleep timer*
*   *2 sets of composite inputs (1 front and 1 rear), S-video input, RF coaxial input, and headphone jack*

*   *Dual speaker setup (5 watts x 2) with MTS stereo, DBX noise reduction, and SAP*

She's standing in front of the Sony KV-20FV10 20" WEGA TV with FD Trinitron picture tube. She's eating a bowl of Whole Earth Organic Corn Flakes, holding the bowl with one hand, spooning the cornflakes with the other. She's feeling numb. This is what comes after the anger and the hurt. Numbness. You stop thinking, you stop feeling, you concentrate on spooning cornflakes into your mouth and on being careful not to spill the cornflakes or the milk onto your clothes. These are the things you can deal with. These are the things that can absorb your attention.

Working with kids she is used to getting messy. It is not that she is mess-averse. But she likes to start the day neat.

The aftermath of an earthquake fills the screen of the KV-20FV10.

The death toll in the Izmit earthquake has reached ten thousand. Many more are missing, trapped inside the rubble of collapsed buildings. The earthquake, which measured 7.8 on the Richter scale, has devastated a number of towns in a highly populated area of Western Turkey.

He will come in and point to this and say, Look, it's as I said. The world is a terrible place. How can you want to bring children into this?

She feels a rekindling of her anger, a vague resentment is all it is. It is something. It is better than numbness. But she ends up hating herself.

She will have no answer for him. She hates herself, is angry with herself, because she's looking at scenes of devastation and ruin and she is unmoved except to feel a vague resentment. It is as if, she is hard on herself as she thinks of this as if, but it is as if she believes the earthquake has been arranged to annoy her, to put her at a disadvantage in her argument with her boyfriend. For they are only boyfriend and girlfriend, they are not married, she is aware of this, and this also undermines her and therefore rekindles her anger. She judges herself to be selfish and petty. Ten thousand people have died and she can only see this catastrophe in terms of how it affects her. It comes down to he will not marry her. They are coming to the point where he will not marry her. And the earthquake in Turkey is not helping.

She is moving through resentment into something more tearful.

She hears the front door, his steps on the stairs, she hears the door to the flat slam. He's in the room with her, panting hard. She does not look at him. But something strange, he goes straight for the phone. He's on the phone.

Hello, yes, Police.

She has to look at him now and he mouths, Turn it down. And gestures with his hand, a patting of the air, down.

She hits mute.

Yeah, hi, yeah. Uh, I don't really know how to put this but, uh, I just found a dead body.

He's looking at her as he says this, looking at her and nodding, grimly, maliciously even, as she chokes on her cornflakes and coughs cornflakes and milk all over her top. And there is something, satisfaction or something, in his eyes.

40. The BODYARMOUR UK Police Concealable Body Armour vest

There is something he can't put his finger on about the guy. It's in the eyes. It could be fear. It stands to reason the guy's afraid. Scared shitless, probably. Who wouldn't be? It's not every day his kind comes across shit like this. His kind being the kind that wears a suit and carries a briefcase, that sits at a desk all day, pushing pens. Nice suit by the way, he thinks but does not say. The guy does not want to know his suit is admired. The guy would not know what to do with the information that the DI on the scene admires his suit. It is professional admiration. From one suit-wearer to another.

Poor fucker though. Why wouldn't he be scared? He came this close to some hammer-happy psycho. He looks like a boy. He has little boy scared eyes. But there's something else there too, something other than fear.

I can understand the fear, Barry thinks. After all, the guy does not have the benefit of a BODYARMOUR UK Police Concealable Body Armour vest. Of course, it has to be said, a BODYARMOUR UK Police Concealable Body Armour vest, safe as it makes you feel, would not be much use in the event of a hammer-wielding nutcase coming at you from behind a tree.

So what do you do? he feels the need to ask.

He finds it hard to imagine what people do, but important to know. For instance, he cannot, this guy, no one can, sit at a desk all day literally pushing pens. Not literally. He knows that it is not meant literally, but that is the image that persists. This guy in his suit, nice suit, sitting at a desk, literally pushing pens off the edge of his desk. There must be more to it than that. No one would pay you to do that all day. It must involve computers.

Sometimes he thinks all he'd like to do is watch what people do all day.

I'm in marketing, the guy answers. His face shows he's shocked by the question but he answers all the same. Takes his time, thinks Barry.

Involve computers? He makes the question sound nonchalant, like he knows full well it involves computers. Why would it not involve computers?

The guy frowns and nods.

Barry nods too. It's like he thought, it involves computers.

So, he says, you were running along where? Here?

The guy nods and it's there in his eyes, the fear, or the something other than fear. Maybe it isn't fear. It's something.

Time?

The guy blows out his cheeks. I don't exactly. Some time after six. I set the alarm for six. Get straight up and go for my run.

Shower when you get back? Barry wants to know this. It doesn't have any direct bearing on the case but he wants to know. He is good at what he does because, basically, he is nosey. He knows this. He says this often. You know why I'm such a good cop? he often says. Because I'm nosey. It's the perfect job for a nosey bastard like me.

Yes, the guy says.

You went back for a shower today? He makes it sound pointed.

I went back to call the police. To call you.

And then you had a shower?

What should I have done? The guy is getting antsy. There are no payphones anymore, he says it as if this is Barry's fault. I didn't have my mobile. Obviously.

Could have knocked on someone's door.

I didn't think. Besides it isn't that far to my flat. My girlfriend. The guy doesn't finish.

His girlfriend what? thinks Barry. He says, Nice flat by the way. What he's thinking is, Nice girlfriend.

The guy makes no comment. It's like he resents that they came round to the flat, that they insisted on picking him up so he could show them where exactly he found what he found. But of course, what else are they going to do? What did he expect?

You saw the body from over here? Barry makes his voice sound incredulous. He wants to find out what it is about the guy's eyes. He wants to get to the bottom of the thing about the guy's eyes.

No, I saw the dog first.

Oh yes, the dog. Barry looks at the dog. The dog is fucking tragic. The dog is unnecessary. The dog is sadistic. The dog, this killing of the dog, is something else. A joke comes into his mind. You could call it a joke. He will not say it but he cannot help it coming into his mind. Why did the psycho kill the dog? Because he didn't want any witnesses.

He looks at the guy and wonders if he is the sort who would find that funny. Probably not. Not now, not today, not in the circumstances. If the guy wasn't there he'd share the joke, if you can call it a joke, with the uniforms. It's the sort of thing they'd appreciate.

So you saw the dog. Then what?

I saw something move. Over there. Where the body is.

Barry can't help himself. He exchanges a look with one of the uniforms, DC Carter. So Johnny was still hanging around is what the look says. They understand this. The something moving. Johnny. That's what the look between them means.

The guy must have seen it, the look between Barry and the uniform.

What? he wants to know.

They are not going to share the meaning of that look. It is not for him to know the meaning of that look. Why put him through it?

A bird? A bird taking off? Barry suggests. He manages to empty his voice of conviction.

I didn't see a bird, says the guy. He's watching them closely, watching Barry and the uniforms. You did it again, he says. That look. What does it mean, that look? You think it was the murderer. You think he was still there, watching me?

Barry feels the BODYARMOUR UK Police Concealable Body Armour vest cling comfortably to his skin. He feels the padded sections around his midriff. He feels the velcro straps over his shoulders. He feels himself in its grip and yes he knows it's no use against a hammer in the head but wearing it lets him understand the fear of one who doesn't have the privilege. Who has nothing.

The World's most popular style of undershirt vest.

Six point velcro adjustable ensures a smooth comfortable fit.

Front, back and side protected as standard. Specifically designed to withstand the rigours of military and tactical service life. The vest is tough, durable, easy to don and doff and a well proven style.

Many thousands of these vests are in current active service.

The selection of materials, ergonomic design and structure of the garment ensure longevity.

He sees the guy lift his briefcase as though that will protect him.

The chances are he was running away, says Barry. He knows how to make his voice sound as he makes these pronouncements. He can do authoritative. He can look the guy steadily in the eye as he says this. He probably didn't wait to get a look at you, he says.

At the last, he flinches his gaze away. He finds it hard to lie but doubts the guy will notice.

Forensics are cordoning off the crime scene. They have the tape. They have the tent.

Nice suit, says Barry. He wants to make the guy feel better. Can't stop himself being nosey though, You have to wear a suit for work?

Yes. No. Sometimes.

The guy has his head cocked as he looks around.

Do you think he's still here? In the woods. Do you think he could be still here?

That is unlikely. Did you touch the body?

No. The guy says it quickly and adds quickly, Why would I touch the body?

Barry gives a shrug. It's a question we ask, he says. You'd be surprised. Some people, he says. He watches the guy as he looks around.

I didn't touch it, says the guy.

Barry nods. OK, he says. You can go. We know where you are if we need you.

The guy nods. Barry nods. The guy nods. He nods and turns and tears himself away.

I wonder what he has in the briefcase, comes into Barry's mind for no reason. But he lets the guy go. He wants to know what's in the briefcase but he lets the guy go.

41. The Initial 2-Fold Hand Towel

He has the Twirl mug. She comes into the kitchen and sees that he's taking the Twirl mug out of the cupboard. She doesn't say anything. She watches him put the Twirl mug down heavily. Steady, she thinks. Careful with my mug, she thinks. But she doesn't say anything. She watches. She watches him spoon Nescafé into the Twirl mug. He has not noticed her. He must know there's someone there, he must be aware of someone out of the corner of his eye, but he doesn't turn to see who. Antisocial bastard, she thinks. She sees the kettle boil. She sees him start to pour the water into the Twirl mug. Funny how she does not expect the Twirl mug to melt when someone else pours. He's holding the Twirl mug with one hand and the kettle with the other. He doesn't need to hold the Twirl mug but he is. And there is something desperate, she senses something desperate, about the way he clings on to the mug. As if the mug is all that's holding him up. As if he has to hold onto the mug, or something, to stop from falling over.

That's my mug, she says. She waits till now to say this. It's a joke, she's joking, but her voice sounds stern. To make this kind of joke work you have to keep your voice stern, you have to sound like you mean it.

His hand, the hand that's holding the Twirl mug, shakes. The Twirl mug clatters on the work surface, spilling hot Nescafé over the work surface and over his hand.

Fuck, he says.

Run it under the tap, she tells him. She goes to the sink and gets the cold tap running. Run it under the tap, she insists.

He does as he is told.

I'm sorry, he says. He's looking down at his hand in the water stream and so is she.

Why? she wants to know.

For taking your mug.

I was only joking.

She watches the water play around his hand.

Berk, she adds after watching the water play around his hand for a while. He looks up. She looks into his eyes. They look into each other's eyes.

He gives that kind of smiling sigh that is almost a laugh.

You're very hard, he says.

How is it? she asks.

He looks down at his hand, as if he can only tell by looking at it.

Cold, he says.

You have to keep it there for ten minutes.

I can't stand here holding my hand under a tap for ten minutes. I've already been bollocked by Tony.

Why?

Late.

Again? She should have perhaps tried harder to keep the surprise out of her voice.

Oh, great.

No, I mean, I know you were late on your first day. It stuck in my mind.

And mine.

What was it this morning?

He looks up, looks for her eyes. She gives him her gaze.

You don't want to know, he says. And it is said simply, a statement of fact. There is little rhetoric at play. He keeps his gaze steady.

OK, she says.

He does not seem inclined to offer more.

She gets an Initial paper hand towel from the Initial dispenser and moves the spilt coffee around with it.

Initial 2-Fold Hand Towel White 1 Ply

Please leave this kitchen in the state you would wish to find it, she recites, without looking at the sellotaped notice.

You're very good, he says.

She throws the first Initial paper hand towel away and pulls out a bundle of others. The Initial dispenser makes a noise like it's clearing its throat as each Initial paper hand towel is taken out.

No, she says. I'm very bad.

She keeps her face straight. She puts everything she's feeling into her eyes. She wonders if he picks up on this. He's looking into her eyes so maybe he does.

She's standing next to him at the sink.

Can I? she says, holding one of the Initial paper hand towels towards the running water.

I thought I had to keep it here for ten minutes, he teases.

I only want to wet it.

He takes his hand out of the water. The water hammers the stainless steel sink.

Go ahead.

She passes the Initial paper hand towel through the water stream.

How's it feel? she asks.

Wet.

You can put it back in if you want.

It's OK.

D'you want one of these?

He takes one of the dry Initial paper hand towels. He wraps it round his hand like a bandage.

The reason I was late, he says.

She turns away from him, gets on with mopping up the coffee. There's something about his tone that she doesn't want to face.

You wouldn't believe it.

Try me, she says.

I found a dead body in the woods.

No.

She feels the air enter her. It is not simply breathing. It is a gust of air entering her. She becomes airborne for an instant, at the instant the air enters her. The awareness of being alive, she has never had this sense of her own air-sustained living.

Yes. I was out running, my normal morning run through Queen's Wood. And I saw this... well, actually at first, I saw the dog. The dog was lying there, dead. Then I saw something move. The police think it could have been the murderer.

The murderer?

Yes.

Jesus, Rob.

I was looking for the dog's owner. I thought the dog's owner, maybe it was the dog's owner. The dog's head was smashed in. I thought, I didn't know. I went towards it. I saw something move and went towards it. And there he was. Lying on the ground, the owner, the dog's owner. And he was the same. His head was smashed in, the same. He was dead, the same. And the funny thing was. I saw him yesterday. I see him every day and he never lets on to me. He never has once.

There are tears now coming from his eyes. She is looking into his eyes and she sees the tears coming from them.

She reaches one of the Initial paper hand towels towards his face and wipes the tears away.

I'm with someone, he says.

I know. Julia.

You're with someone, he says.

She screws the Initial paper hand towel up and crosses to the bin. She is glad to be able to turn her back on him and for it to appear natural. She releases the pop-up lid and drops the Initial paper hand towel into the bin.

Then turns to face him. I don't have to be, she says.

42. The Bic biro

The children are at her feet. She sits on the chair and they sit on the carpet, there is an area of carpet at the front of the classroom. She holds their attention with a biro, an ordinary Bic biro, clear plastic, pierced by a black vein of sluggish ink. She holds the Bic between the tips of her thumb and forefinger. She holds it steady. They cannot take their eyes off it. It is a trick she has taught herself to do, a kind of hypnotism. They are good kids but sometimes a wild excitement will pass through them, a collective convulsion. She calls these her forest fire days. It is impossible to say what sets it off. She sits them down on the carpet. Right everybody, she will say, and she has a way of making her voice carry over their excitement. Right everybody, carpet. She'll have the Bic biro in her hand ready. She'll be holding it ready in front of her like a conductor with a baton. She will wait without speaking, just holding the Bic, for them to take their places on the carpet, they all know where they must sit. It is not random. Each child knows who they should be next to or behind. And they will busy themselves with this sitting down, with finding their unmarked places, working out their places in relation to one another. It is enough this activity, this sitting down on the carpet, to distract them from their strange excitement. And she will not have to say a thing. She will watch them sitting down. Another trick she has taught herself is to keep her eyes wide open, to make her eyes appear as big as they can in her face, to emphasise the watching. She signals watching with her whole face. They feel her watching as they take their places. She focuses on giving each one of them a portion of this watching, on making sure that each one of them feels the watching. As they sort out their places they will notice the Bic biro. Their attention will be held by the Bic biro. Perhaps they are wondering, Why is she holding that biro? What is she going to do with that biro? Or perhaps, more likely, it doesn't get to that, the formation of questions. It is just something you can't help doing if you are a six year old child. If someone holds a Bic biro in front of them, out to you, you have to look at it. The thing is it works. It's a trick she has taught herself and it works.

Perhaps it is just that she has confidence to hold the Bic and believe in the Bic.

Sometimes it can be the weather, the wind in the trees, the sound of the wind in the trees, that sets them off. The wild shaking of branches and leaves seems contagious. Other times she wonders if it is something to do with the phases of the moon. They are like little werewolves. She has never set herself to prove this one way or the other. She has no interest in proving it one way or the other.

When they are at last all quiet, and still, their attention fixed on the Bic biro, she will begin. Listen everybody, listen to me. And it is a kind of hypnotism. She doesn't know anything about hypnotism but she has worked this out for herself. She has found that talking to them like this works. Talking slowly, clearly, stating the obvious, repeating the obvious. They become gripped by her words, they listen. Even the difficult ones. Harry who is autistic spectrum. Oliver who is ADHD. Ali who has no label to his behaviour, who is simply exuberant, who cannot control the tumble of words from his mouth, if he thinks something he says it, there is no filter with that boy. Even he is staring at the Bic biro.

Of course, it will not last forever, this holding them rapt with a Bic biro. She only has a few seconds at most. But a few seconds of having the whole class, all twenty nine of them, fixed on a Bic biro in her hand is worth a lot. A few seconds fixed on a Bic biro is a marvel.

She wonders, would it work with them next year, when they are Year Two? Or is there just this window of susceptibility?

Right everybody, she says. She has judged that it is time for the words to begin. She cannot hold them with the biro alone forever. Who can tell me why I've got you sitting on the carpet? Why did I ask you to sit on the carpet? What were you doing? What was happening? Can anybody tell me?

It is a big class but there are no bad ones. Sometimes there is inappropriate behaviour. But they will all sit and watch the Bic biro, at least for a few seconds. They will all sit and puzzle out the reason why she has called them to the carpet.

43. The Google search engine

He has the Twirl mug on the Unifor i Satelliti S200 desk. He has the monitor platform raised to eye level. He's sitting straight up in his chair, looking straight at the IBM ThinkVision L170P flat panel monitor. There is no hunching. His back is straight. His head position is good. He is comfortable. He has never been so comfortable looking at a monitor. The monitor platform is a miracle. The monitor platform is a piece of genius. The Twirl mug is on one level, hand level you could call it. The IBM ThinkVision L170P is on another, eye level, naturally, of course. It's simple, it's obvious but it works.

On a third level, out of sight, on the floor beneath the Unifor i Satelliti S200 is the Di Beradino classic.

Inside the Di Beradino classic: the Snoopy ring binder, the Benjys napkin with the dumped girl's tears, the generic handkerchief with the Securicor security guard's blood, and now there is also the enamel badge with the brass letters NLHS taken from the man with his head smashed in. There is also, in another compartment, the letter to Mrs Emily Green. He has yet to send the letter to Mrs Emily Green. His current paperback is in there too but no bananas today. Somehow today the bananas were overlooked.

He feels the importance and the power of the objects he has taken. He feels the sense of balance, of balance restored, provided by the letter to Mrs Emily Green. It is there in its potential to be sent. He can send the letter, one day perhaps he will send the letter, and it will make amends. In the meantime he carries around his intention.

He is comfortable with XP. He clicks on the Internet Explorer icon, the soft moulded blue e with the orbiting ring around it. His browser opens on Guardian Unlimited. He has set his Internet Options so that Guardian Unlimited is his default home page.

He reads in the rolling headline panel that the death toll in Turkey has reached ten thousand. And then the ten thousand dead are gone. Another piece of news rolls into view.

He thinks about what the policeman said, the CID officer, Detective Inspector Barry Griffith is his name. Does it involve computers? he said. He said a lot of other things but Rob thinks only about this. Does it involve computers?

He overtypes google.co.uk into the URL address box. He prefers the .co.uk version of Google to the .com version because he can set it to search only UK sites or he can set it to search the whole web, the worldwide web. He has been tasked, he feels he can use that word because it is an American, Morello, he has been tasked to draw up a long list of agencies. Inevitably they will be UK agencies so the facility of selecting only UK sites will come into its own.

He has the brightly coloured letters of the Google UK logo on the IBM ThinkVision L170P flat panel monitor. The brightly coloured letters are surrounded by soothing, comforting white.

He types the word disasters, he does not uppercase the initial d, he types disasters into the elongated box. It has come to this. He should be drawing up a list of agencies but he types the word disasters.

There are options now. He can click the Google search button or he can click I'm feeling lucky. He can select the web or he can select pages from the UK.

He is not feeling lucky. He has never favoured the I'm feeling lucky option. He selects the web and clicks Google Search.

It is almost instant, the list appears almost instantly. On a human scale, it is instant.

Results 1 - 10 of about 2,770,000 for disasters. (0.21 seconds)

Top of the list is AirDisaster.com. Second is Airline Disasters. The third is FEMA for KIDS Homepage: Education, Schools, Disasters, Games. He is for some reason curious about this site. He reads the descriptor, This site teaches you how to be prepared for disasters and how you can prevent disaster damage. ... Disasters aren't fun, but learning about them is! ... www.fema.gov/kids/ - 6k - Cached - Similar pages.

He resists opening any of the first ten results. It is too overwhelming. Two million seven hundred and seventy thousand results. He doesn't have time to look through two million seven hundred and seventy thousand results. He is supposed to be drawing up a long list of agencies. He is supposed to be looking at agencies' web sites.

He goes back to the google.co.uk home page, to the big colourful letters in the white space.

He selects from the UK and hits I'm feeling lucky.

The site it gives him, dangerousworld.co.uk.

The graphics of the site are the first disaster. As a marketing man, he cannot help thinking this. The design is a disaster. It was always going to be. It comforts him, somehow it comforts him, that he is able to think this. He is not so far gone after all. He still notices bad design. He still takes time to make a joke about it. What a fucking disaster, he thinks, meaning the design.

The background is blue and there is blocky arial type in green coming out of the blue. There is random italicising and there is mixed type sizes. There is no discernible layout grid. There is everything all over the place. There are little green and blue world graphics, the land masses in green the seas in blue, a slightly different blue from the background.

There is a blurred black and white photograph of wreckage, the wreckage of a crashed airliner. The photograph was taken inside the cabin. He can see the mangled seats and the shell of the cabin ripped open. He spends some time looking at this photograph. There are no bodies that he can see. It must have been taken after the bodies were taken away.

It has come to this.

The photograph, he realises, is a come-on.

The blues clash, the blue of the background and the blue of the oceans in the little world graphics. The little worlds bulletpoint the headings of the site contents menu.

DISASTERS BY DEATH TOLL
DISASTERS BY TYPE (FIRE, EARTHQUAKE, AIR, OTHER)
DISASTERS BY LOCATION
DISASTERS BY DATE
RANDOM DISASTER GENERATOR

ACTS OF TERROR
SOUVENIRS

It has come to this, his heart quickening with a tense, pre-sweaty, illicit excitement as he sees the site has a souvenirs page. He is intrigued by the random disaster generator, but his cursor goes first for the souvenirs heading.

Before he can click, the shock of a voice at his back.

Busy?

He makes the cursor fly to the task bar at the bottom of the screen. He has a hidden document sitting in the task bar tagged with a word icon, the blue w on a minuscule graphic page. He clicks to bring the w tagged document out from its hiding place.

What the hell was that you were looking at? It's Tony standing over him.

Oh, it's just some background research I was doing.

On what?

I've got some ideas. They're pretty sketchy. To do with the world. You know, what people are afraid of. What makes them feel insecure.

Uh, so you're coming up with the fucking creative work now, are you?

No. It's just, I though we could feed it into the brief.

It's a bit early days for that, sunshine. Fucking hell. Tony shakes his head. I suppose I should be thankful you weren't downloading kiddy porn. Mind you, somehow. Tony is still shaking his head. There is something deliberate about the way he is still shaking his head. Maybe that was worse, he says.

Tony's staring at the document Rob has open, DIAMOND LIFE STAFF CONTACT NUMBERS. He's stopped shaking his head now. How you getting on? he says. With the long list?

Fine. Yeah. Good.

So when am I going to see something?

Soon.

How soon?

Very soon.

Today?

I've only really been working on it one day. I haven't had all the stuff from the AAR.

Tomorrow?

Maybe. I don't know. Al Morello didn't mention a deadline.

I'm your line manager, not Morello.

Of course.

You would have got further if you hadn't been late in this morning. Perhaps you should try getting out of bed a bit earlier in the morning.

I get up at six.

It's obviously not early enough, is it.

No, says Rob. He's thinking about telling Tony about the dead man in the woods but decides against it. He had his chance earlier. It will seem odd now.

You're going to have to put in the hours on this.

I'm prepared to do that. Naturally. This morning was, uh, not typical, I promise you.

So, says Tony, nodding at the document open on the IBM ThinkVision L170P. Whose mobile number are you after? To Rob's relief, he doesn't stay for an answer. It's not a serious question. He's trying lighten the mood, trying to show he's not such a bastard after all. There's even a sly wink as he swivels away.

As soon as Tony is back in his office, he is one of the men with offices, Rob's cursor falls to the task bar at the bottom and he clicks the e tagged dangerousworld.co.uk page.

44. The Yves-rocher Yria Lip Contour Pencil brun

She draws a perfect line. She's been on since eight, half an hour for lunch, but her hand is still steady. Her lips are large in the compact mirror, she's holding the compact mirror right up to her lips, that's how you check someone's still alive, if the mirror mists. The mirror mists. She draws a perfect line with the Yves-rocher Yria Lip Contour Pencil brun.

She knows the importance of hydrating beauty products.

She knows the rhythms of the reception. She's going into a quiet period. It's getting close to four. She leaves at four. The rest of them leave at five, or most of them do. There aren't many visitors in the last hour. Who would have a visitor when you're getting ready to go home?

Now is the time she refreshes the smile. She doesn't need it professionally but she needs it to get her home. Now is a good time to check the smile and sharpen up the outline. To make sure she's good to go.

Yria Make-Up
Lip Contour Pencil brun
Take aim at a beautiful smile.
A retractable pencil with a creamy texture, for emphasizing or correcting the shape of your lips.
pencil 0.28 g

There is an internal. She knows the difference between an internal and an external call of course. This one is internal. The extension number of the caller shows on the display of her M2250 digital attendant console. 3140. Her heart sinks. It's Kelly, the marketing secretary. There can only be one reason she's calling.

Donna moves the compact away from her lips. She presses the key for speakerphone.

Kelly, she says. Her voice is flat. She is still looking at her lips in the mirror of her compact. She is holding the compact at arm's length for the full effect. The line is good. The lips are good.

Donna. She can tell from Kelly's voice what is to come. Donna, love, I can't do it.

But Kelly it's five to four. She watches her lips move as she says this. It is as if someone else is speaking. It is as if she is two people.

It's mad here, Donna. Tony Dawson's just given me a PowerPoint to do. She watches her lips purse as Kelly speaks.

I can't get anyone else now. It's strange to see her own disembodied lips speaking. She feels like she is miming.

Have you tried Sheena?

Well no. I haven't tried anyone, have I? You've only just told me. I'll have to do it myself. She admires the settling symmetry of her lips, the perfection of the line.

You could try Sheena or Moni.

It's too late, Kelly. I can't expect people to do it without any notice. How quick her lips can move. How crisp the line remains.

I'm sorry, Donna. I thought I was going to be OK.

You've got to let me know earlier. She wants to keep the conversation going so she can keep watching her lips.

I'm sorry. Like I said, I thought I was going to be OK. He's only just dumped this on me.

And now she is watching her lips as they do not speak, as they remain crisp and clamped together. She watches her own anger compressed in her lips. And knows that there is something artificial about her anger.

Donna?

I have to go. It is a lie. She wonders why she said it. Was it just to see its shape, the shape of a lie, on her lips?

She presses the speakerphone key to end the call. And with one hand folds the compact closed over her lips. There is the sense that she is catching her lips in the closing compact. That her lips, the reflection of her lips is a marvellous butterfly she has trapped.

She still has the Yves-rocher Yria Lip Contour Pencil brun in the other hand.

She looks at the tree, the atrium tree, as if only the tree can understand. She is to some degree calmed by the tree and consoled.

Her gaze is drawn by movement in the revolving door. She watches the revolving door and prepares herself. A dispatch rider, she thinks, it will be a dispatch rider at this time. Cycle or motorbike? She plays the game with herself. Cycle or motorbike? But it is neither. It is not a dispatch rider at all. It is some kind of workman. It is a man in scruffy clothes, a thickset man with the hood of his top pulled up over his head. She thinks he is some kind of workman because he has a hammer in his hand, one of those metal hammers that workmen use. He doesn't approach the reception desk. He stays near the revolving door. He's looking around, like he's weighing the place up for some kind of job he is about to do. He looks at the tree. He spends some time looking at the tree. But he doesn't look at Donna.

Can I help you? she calls out.

Still he doesn't look in her direction.

Excuse me, she calls again. There is something about him, maybe it is the hood pulled up. But there is something she doesn't like, something that doesn't feel right.

Finally he turns his head in her direction, though his eyes do not look for hers. He mumbles something she doesn't catch and goes out through the revolving door.

She puts the compact down on the reception desk. She retracts and lids the Yves-rocher Yria Lip Contour Pencil brun, puts it on the desk next to the compact. She reaches for the Evian Natural Spring Water 0.75l Nomad bottle. She holds the bottle with both hands. She doesn't drink. She doesn't even raise it to her lips. It is just the feel of the Nomad bottle she wants in her hands. She could go to Prague maybe, or Nice. With the Nomad bottle in her hands she has the feeling she could go anywhere.

45. The BT Synergy 3105 cordless digital phone

She feels it building. It will do this. Build. But it will never overwhelm her. She will feel it build and she will be able to hold it at bay. There will come a point when she feels it's going to overwhelm her when she can hold it no longer, she feels. But it never does. She knows, when she feels herself reaching that point, she knows what she must do. She knows she must hold it at bay for a little longer. She knows she must not give in to it yet. She knows she must not call Julia yet. But she knows she is close to the point when she will, when she can allow herself to call Julia. And knowing this reassures her. It is one of the things that help her keep it at bay. Thinking about calling Julia is one of the things that help her put off the moment when she needs to call Julia.

This is how she deals with her fear.

She is a sensible woman and strong.

Sitting in the garden helps. Holding the phone helps. Sitting in the garden holding the phone, the handset of the cordless phone that Julia and Rob bought her so she can have the phone near her while she's in the garden, so she doesn't have to come in from the garden to answer the phone. It is typical of Julia to think of this, to understand without anything having to be explained that this gift would help, that this is the one gift that will help.

So it helps to have the phone on her lap while she is sitting in the garden. Because the phone, even just holding the phone in her lap, brings her closer to Julia, she doesn't even have to call her to feel herself closer to her, and holding the phone in the garden is best of all, because she is completing the thought, it was Julia's thought, Julia's idea, and she feels she is playing her part in completing it.

BT Synergy 3105
A digital cordless you can use handsfree

And the phone will ring sometimes when she least expects it and it will be Julia or it will not be Julia. But the phone will be there in her lap and she can answer it straight away and whoever it is she will feel a little less afraid.

You have to press the button with the little green telephone on it to start talking.

People will call her and sometimes it will be Julia and sometimes it will not be Julia but Julia is the only one she will call when she feels she can't hold the fear at bay any longer.

If you can't call your own daughter who can you call?

But Julia has her own life now, she knows that. She is a sensible woman.

So she puts off the moment when she calls for as long as she can. She contents herself with the phone in her lap, with thinking of Julia, with the thought that when it gets too much she can enter Julia's number so that Julia's number shows on the display. And sometimes she will press the button with the little telephone on it and sometimes she will wait a little longer and perhaps the need to make the call will go.

And what will give her strength, and what will give her courage most of all is that she is still protecting Julia, that she still has a way of protecting her daughter from the worst that can happen. And that is simply to call her and keep the fear from her voice, to talk of the clematis and the rosemary how the rosemary is taking over, you wouldn't believe it. To sit in the garden and talk of the garden. To keep the fear from her voice and to talk only of the things that are growing in the garden and not of the fear that is growing inside her.

46. The Ikea Grundtal dish drainer

There is always this thing, she thinks, the night after you've been out for a meal. It's like the piquing of grief she gets from the Marvelon foil topped plastic dispenser, the way it pops out the days inescapably. The way it reminds her, This is your life, these are the days of your life. There is time off for good behaviour. Her chemically regulated period is her holiday from the Marvelon tyranny. Eating out is her holiday from the kitchen.

The strange thing is, she likes it, in this case she likes the getting back to normal. She wants the routine. She wants the return. She wants her life to be something unexceptional that pulls at her. There will be holidays from it, little holidays that she will enjoy, but the main thing is she wants the days, she wants to feel herself in the days, she wants to make peace with the days. How can you escape from them? It's a mistake to want that. They are the point, this is the point, coming back into the kitchen, looking at the unwashed mugs and pots, the dishes, the clutter that you have to face. Feeling it pull at you, but feeling also, It's OK if it pulls at me. Let it pull at me. This is where I am. This is my life.

It's just the Marvelon dispenser she doesn't want.

She's happy to set the hot tap running. She's happy to squeeze in the Sainsbury's Spring Fresh washing up liquid. She's happy to watch the bubbles build.

It's mostly mugs. The mugs build up and the glasses. And there are breakfast things. Her bowl, his plate. She loads the dishes into the sink as it fills. They don't have a washing up bowl. She washes up directly in the sink. The sink is stainless steel though the irony is it stains very easily. She adds a little more of the Sainsbury's Spring Fresh washing up liquid. She likes this moment, this moment of fresh bubbles submerging dirty dishes. She can put her hands in the bubbles, but below the bubbles is too hot.

Over the draining board, mounted on the wall, there's the stainless steel draining rack they bought from Ikea, the Grundtal dish drainer.

Saves space on the countertop.
Can be hung on GRUNDTAL mounting strip or on the wall.
May also be used in high humidity areas.
Combines with other accessories in the GRUNDTAL series
designer: Mikael Warnhammar

The Grundtal dish drainer is already stacked with clean dry plates and there are a couple of mugs on there too. The first thing she must do is clear the Grundtal dish drainer. She dries her hands. She takes the clean dry plates out one by one and puts them away in the cupboard. She is brisk and efficient. The taking of plates from the Grundtal dish drainer, the putting away, this is her life. She will be content with it. This is why you take trouble over choosing every object, even utilitarian objects like a dish drainer. She could have bought a cheap plastic one from Woolworths, one that just sits on the worktop, but she chose the Grundtal wall-mounted dish drainer from Ikea. It pleases her. It is one of the objects that make up her life. She chose it well. She likes that it's stainless steel. She likes that it's wall-mounted. She likes that it's Ikea. She likes that there is someone who designed it, that there is the name of the person who designed it. It makes up for a lot, to have a dish drainer that pleases you.

Maybe she is mad to think like this. Maybe I am mad, she thinks. In the same way that maybe she is mad to want a baby. Maybe the two things are connected. One madness is the child of the other. Or maybe it just means she's ready.

She's happy to be here alone in the kitchen, taking white Ikea plates one by one from the Grundtal dish drainer. She's happy he's not back yet, happy he's working late, or whatever he's doing, yes, she even thinks that, whatever he's doing. She's happy he's not there to complicate this moment. She knows he's not ready, she knows he will resent the dishes even though she's the one dealing with them. Leave them, he would say. Why are you doing them now? He hates the return to normal. If it was down to him they would eat out every night. If it was down to him, they would have a dishwasher, an Ariston, a Braun or a GEC. He has even looked into brands but it's madness, they don't have the space. That's his solution to everything, to look into brands.

You can have a dishwasher if I can have a baby. This is what she will say to him.

She remembers his face when he was on the phone to the police. She wonders, not entirely seriously but still the thought comes into her head, she wonders if the whole thing, the finding of the body, was arranged to teach her a lesson, to make some kind of point.

It is a bitter thought but it comforts.

She has cleared the Grundtal and taken the pans off the draining board below. She plunges her hands beneath the bubbles into the too hot water. She holds them there.

Being a teacher comes into it too. You cannot escape the passage of time when you are a teacher. The year is divided up and marked off in terms and half terms. The terms and half terms accumulate. The years accumulate. This is her life. This is how her life is measured, by terms and half terms and Marvelon dispensers. The children grow up. They pass through the school. You watch the years pass as the children you have taught move up and through the school. She has been a teacher for ten years. The first children she taught, her first Year One class, will be sixteen now. The age of consent. The age of Marvelon. But even in the year she has them for, even in the year they are hers, they grow up. They grow up and move away from her. Every term they change. Every half term.

She has her hands in the hot water. The salt of her skin is reacting with the bubbles. The moment of the bubbles' ascendancy never lasts. They are starting to pop already. She thinks of her mother. Why now does she think of her mother as the bubbles start to pop? She can project backwards and forwards to put herself at any point in her mother's life.

She wipes the first mug round with the Budgens Non-Stick Sponge Scourer. She uses the white abrasive side to scour the tea stains in the mug. The tea stains transfer from the mug to the white fibres of the scourer. It is a stage in the decay of the scourer. She places the mug on the Grundtal dish drainer. The soapy water drips down.

She hears the phone ring. She has a premonition that it will be her mother.

47. The Starbucks Coffee cardboard cup

He can't remember when he lost his shoes. With each step, he splits the skin of his feet in a new place. The pain from his feet tightens his face. He knows they look at his feet. He knows they look at him. They put their hands over their mouths and noses and look at him and move away.

He's dressed in four layers of clothes. They are all the clothes he has. They are everything he has. The first layer of clothes are the clothes he was wearing the day he began walking. The others were taken from bags abandoned in the doorways of charity shops. There is a tremendous urge to put shoes over the feet, but no good reason. Shoes over the feet won't help. They will only bring new pains. The nails. The nails hurt when he puts on shoes. He doesn't want any more new pains. He already has the new pain in the left eye. There is a new pain in the left eye. But the urge to cover the feet in shoes is strong.

He sticks to the City. The Square Mile, they call it. It is his home now, the nearest thing he has to a home. He can go anywhere he wants but he sticks to the City. Round the Old Street Roundabout. The southern stretch of the City Road. On to Finsbury Pavement, Moorgate. Then right into London Wall. Then north again where London Wall becomes Wormwood, north there along Old Broad Street, into Liverpool Street. That is his route today. That is his route every day.

And every time he looks at Liverpool Street station he weeps. When he gets to Liverpool Street station he straightens his bent aching back and weeps. He cannot bear to look at Liverpool Street station for long.

He takes it slowly, on account of the feet, on account of the emphysema and on account of this is how he takes it, slowly. He is not going anywhere. And the City is not going anywhere. And on account of the pains.

There is a new pain today. A pain in his left eye. He's not seeing too well out of the left eye today. There is a reason for it, he thinks, but he can't remember the reason for it. The pain doesn't trouble him, but the newness of it does. He wants to reach a place where the pain doesn't feel new any more. He will reach a place and the pain will join all the other pains, the other pains will welcome it, Hello brother, the other pains will say. Welcome to your new abode, such as it is. Or other some such nonsense. He does not know how pains communicate. He feels sure that they communicate. It will not be through language, human language, though perhaps it might be. There will have to be some sort of transmitter. If only he could talk to this new pain. He would ask it, How did I get you? Or he would let his other pains ask it, Where did you come from, Brother? Whence. Perhaps they will say whence. He feels that the language of pains will be old-fashioned to some degree.

He feels that he is approaching Liverpool Street station. He feels the weeping coming on. Sometimes it is too much. Sometimes he can't bear to straighten his bent aching back. Sometimes he can't bear to look at it. He will turn east on Liverpool Street, he will put the station behind him and he will keep his eyes fixed on his bloody scabby feet.

He feels the weeping well up and knows that today will be one of those days when he cannot look at Liverpool Street station.

The station is there, aglow with emotion. He knows it is there. He feels its glow, its presence, but he will not look at it. It will be too much. He turns east in Liverpool Street and feels the station's massive presence at his back.

And with his head down, watching his shuffling scabby bloody filthy feet, oh how he wishes he had some shoes to cover them, oh, for decency's sake, to cover those vile nails, fuck the pain, fuck whatever pain it causes him, he would kill for a pair of shoes to hide his shame, and with his head down, he sees it, a cardboard cup, it is a cardboard cup, and it has the words Starbucks Coffee on the side. The words Starbucks Coffee are in a green roundel around the illustration of a female figure, a mermaid could it be, for some reason he thinks it is a mermaid or something mythical, she is wearing a crown. He sees his ugly toe kick against the Starbucks Coffee cardboard cup, sending the crowned female flying.

He hears a small voice cry out from the Starbucks Coffee cardboard cup. He hears the small voice cry out, Cunt.

He lifts the Starbucks Coffee cardboard cup and places it to his ear.

That cunt Spider, it was that cunt Spider. That cunt Spider bottled you in the eye under Blackfriars Bridge last night. It was over a pair of shoes. That cunt Spider nicked your shoes. That cunt Spider said you never wear them so he was going to have them. And when you tried to get them back off him, the cunt smashed a bottle and thrust it jagged end first in your eye.

He stops at the corner of Liverpool Street and Blomfeld Street. He looks at the Starbucks Coffee cardboard cup in wonder. He puts the Starbucks Coffee cardboard cup to his ear again.

It is a different voice.

Ten thousand people now. Ten thousand people. Dead. They reckon. Just like that. Ten thousand people dead. Wiped out. Imagine that. Ten thousand people. Who's fault is it? That's what they haven't said. They knew it would happen. They meet. In private. All the leaders. And decide where the next disaster's going to happen. The next earthquake. The next flood. The next war. Today it is Izmit. Tomorrow where will it be? They decide. They still do it, you know. Human sacrifice. You think it went out with the Aztecs? Wrong. They still do it. It's you next. You. You're next. You wait.

He takes the Starbucks Coffee cardboard cup away from his ear and carries on walking. He can still hear the voice in the cup though he can't make out what it's saying. It's like the sound in a telephone when you hold the telephone away from your ear.

He reaches Finsbury Circus. He walks north along Finsbury Circus and now he can feel the voice vibrating in the cup as well as hear it.

He puts the Starbucks Coffee cardboard cup next to his ear. He hears many voices overlapping. The cup is filled with voices. He takes the cup away sharply. If the voices get inside him, if the voices spill from the cup into his ear, pain, the pain of the voices, the voices are the voices of pain and the pain will be inside him.

The voices in the cup are loud. They are drowning out the traffic noises. He is back on Moorgate. There is traffic. But the voices in the cup are drowning out the traffic noises. He hears them only as a roar, the roar of a crowd.

And now the roar of voices merges into one voice, the voice of pain, the voice of the world's pain and it says to him, it says to him clearly so that he can hear it without putting the Starbucks Coffee cardboard cup to his ear, You see this cunt, this cunt in the suit, this cunt in the suit carrying the briefcase. It's you, this cunt. It's how you were. Remember? You were once a cunt in a suit with a briefcase. You had a suit. You had a briefcase. You took the train, remember. You were the cunt in the suit who took the train. Liverpool Street station, remember? You were the cunt in the suit who took the train to Liverpool Street station. The cunt in the suit with the house and the family, two kids, Emily and Katie, remember? You had the house, the family, the wife, the suit, the briefcase, the train. You see this cunt in the suit, that's you, that is.

The cunt in the suit comes towards him. The voice of the world's pain screams at him, Give the cup to the cunt in the suit. Give him the cup, you cunt. Give it to him. The cunt in the suit will know what to do with it.

So he gives the Starbucks Coffee cardboard cup to the cunt in the suit and the cunt in the suit carrying the briefcase takes it off him like he is expecting it, like he knows what to do with it, just as the voices in the cup had said.

And there are tears in his eyes, there are tears in his own eyes, he feels, as he hands the Starbucks Coffee cardboard cup to the cunt.

48. The Pizza Hut pizza delivery trestle

He sits up out of a dream. He has been dreaming of helicopters. The room is filled with the orange glow of flames.

He looks across the bed, across Julia, to the red numerals of the Philips AJ3120 radio alarm clock. 03.30. Julia is sleeping fitfully, murmuring to herself.

The orange glow of flames is no longer there. He wonders if he dreamt it, if it was a residue from his dream.

The sound of a helicopter nearby is still with him. He closes his eyes. The helicopter is so loud it sounds like it's hovering outside their bedroom window.

He slips out of bed. He pulls back the curtain to the window. There is no sign of a helicopter. But the sky is orange. Not the glow of flames: streetlights. He lets the curtain drop.

Julia stirs in the bed.

The door to the bedroom is open. He can see straight through into the living room. The big windows in the living room are flickering squares of orange. The curtains are open. He walks towards the orange squares, passing the Di Beradino classic in the hall. It's there on the floor by the front door where he left it as he came in. It occurs to him that he placed the Di Beradino there as a sentinel, to protect them.

He runs through the contents in his head. The girl suicide's Snoopy ring binder. DON'T ANGER THE GODS' tears on a Benjys napkin. The Securicor security guard's blood on a generic handkerchief. The dead man's badge with the letters NLHS. And now the Starbucks Coffee cardboard cup given him by the weeping tramp. These are the contents he runs through in his head.

It's only now that he thinks it strange, the way the tramp handed him the Starbucks Coffee cardboard cup and the way he took it without questioning. The way they both acted as if this was the most natural thing in the world, as if it was prearranged.

But it had been heading towards this, towards a weeping tramp handing him a Starbucks Coffee cardboard cup. It is as natural as anything else that happens in the world, he thinks.

He crosses the flat to stand at one of the windows in the living room. He looks out at the flaring sky. It is the streetlights but it is something else as well. He can't tell how far away, it seems just a couple of streets away, something is on fire, a building, the roof of a building. The flames are high. A beam of intense white light shoots out from the flames.

The buildings in between are silhouetted by a spreading orange halo. He can hear the sirens now. And the heavy rumble of fire engines shaking the night. They're close. It's close. It could be the next street.

The orange Nike Air Zoom Elite running shoes are in the hall. It seems appropriate that they are orange. Like it's a sign. Or destiny. He is panting as he ties the laces. He looks like he could be going out for a run. He sleeps in shorts and V-neck T-shirt.

He goes back into the bedroom. Julia turns away from him as he comes in. It can only be a coincidence. She is talking in her sleep. He finds his keys.

Back in the hall now, he picks up the Di Beradino classic. It is natural that he should pick up the Di Beradino. It is as natural as anything that happens in the world. He has the hard leather handle in his hand. He's calmed by the touch of the vegetable tanned leather.

He opens and closes the flat door without a sound. He feels his way down the stairs, but the glow through the glass of the front door helps.

As soon as he opens the front door he can taste the smoke in the air. It is that bonfire smell. There are bright little flecks and sparks swirling in the air, like kindled snowflakes.

He squeezes tight on the handle of the Di Beradino classic.

The sound of the helicopter is deafening. He realises that the beam of white light he saw shooting out of the flames is the helicopter's searchlight. The beam of the helicopter is communing with the burning building, drawing something from it. It seems to Rob the helicopter is dangerously low and why is it there anyway? he thinks. Why do you need to shine a searchlight on a burning building?

He jogs towards the beam. The contents of the briefcase jump as he runs. There are more flecks and sparks of fire as he runs. There is more smoke. At one point there is more smoke than air, it seems. His eyes are smarting from the smoke.

He runs into a street filled with fire engines and ambulances and the clatter of the helicopter. The air is suddenly clearer. He has reached the location of the fire, he can see the burning building across the road. But the air is clearer. The smoke and sparks stream upwards in warm currents. The breeze carries them away. The helicopter is directly overhead. He feels the heat of the flames. He can see the building on fire, it's there directly ahead of him, a block of flats. The flames are coming from the top storey, which is to say about the fourth or fifth storey. It's a low rise block of flats, long and low. And the fire is contained at one end of the block. The helicopter seems almost to be sitting on top of the burning building. From the ground it looks like the flames are engulfing the helicopter. There are two engines with aerial platforms in position, the firemen on them spraying constant jets of water into the restless heart of the flames. They are holding the flames in one section of the top storey. He can see this.

There are people in the street and in doorways and looking out of windows of the houses opposite and around. There is a strange excitement in their faces. Some of the people in the street are coughing. But they do not want to move away. The brilliance and proximity of the flames intoxicates. Firemen are shouting at them to get away. They step back a few paces but as soon as the firemen's backs are turned they edge forwards. They know they will never see anything like this again. They are in the street in their dressing gowns and nightwear, it is strange to see what everyone wears in bed, but no one thinks of that now, this is one of those moments of community, of communal intimacy, when such issues do not arise.

The firemen are escorting people out of the block of flats. Paramedics are helping the people into ambulances. There are children clutching teddies. There are old people in pyjamas and nighties. It is terrible and heartbreaking and a privilege also. He feels privileged to be here seeing this.

And there are police there too, he notices. There are police in heavy body armour and black military style helmets. These police are clutching machine guns, the short stubby machine guns that policemen carry. And he is still asking himself the question, Why do you need a spotlight on a burning building, it's not for the firemen, the firefighters should he say, they can see where the burning building is easily enough. Perhaps they are looking for something in the flames, perhaps the searching white light of the beam enables them to see through the flames. It is certainly more brilliant than the flames. Or perhaps the searchlight was on the building before the fire started.

He hears someone in the crowd say that it's terrorists, that they have raided a terrorists' den and something went wrong. Let them burn, someone says. Let the fuckers burn.

He walks past the people who are saying these things and somehow is able to pass between the running firemen and the halting paramedics, the paramedics supporting limping victims, and if it is a man he looks into the man's face and thinks are you a terrorist. He walks, he is able to walk towards the building. He's carrying the Di Beradino. No one challenges him. They are all too busy with what they are doing. They do not expect to see a man walking towards the building and so they do not see him. It must be something like that, he thinks. And it is night and there is smoke billowing out of the building and confusion. And he's carrying the Di Beradino.

And so he walks, he walks towards the billowing smoke, he walks with the steadiness of a man who has the right to be there, to do this. It is more than that. It is with the steadiness of a man who has to be there. And he does not think, he does not once think this is madness.

But there is a fireman at the entrance of the building. A fire officer checking his firemen out, counting them in and counting them out. And it is obvious Rob will not be able to get past him.

There are balconies to the flats, even the ground floor flats have balconies, and he sees that the door to one of these is open.

Possibly it is where someone made their escape, leaving the balcony door open behind them.

The concrete balcony wall is high. He rests the Di Beradino on the balcony wall and pulls himself up to straddle the high concrete balcony wall. He swings the outside leg over and lets himself drop. He is on the balcony and no one has seen him. Everyone is concentrating on the entrance to the flats, on who is coming in and out of there.

At a guess, the block of flats dates from the sixties or seventies. The window and door frames are metal. He touches the metal. The metal is hot. The fire is above him, in the top storey, at the other end of the building, contained in one section of the top storey by the firemen on the aerial platforms. He had thought he would be safe.

But the fire that's visible from the street is only part of the total fire, he realises. It's impossible to say how far the fire has spread inside.

He can go back. It is not too late to clamber back over the high concrete balcony wall. It would be the easiest thing to do. But he cannot take his eyes off the darkness inside for it is dark inside.

He steps through the open door, through the hot metal frame of the balcony door. There is sweat, a layer of sweat, forming between his palm and the handle of the Di Beradino.

It is dark inside and hot. He can see a strip of mutable orange low down. Mutable. Incandescent. He is a marketing man. The smoke is in his throat immediately. It sets him coughing. He pulls the V-neck T-shirt up over his nose and mouth. He remembers something about getting down low. That this is what you should do in a smoke-filled room. He drops to his knees and gets his head down as low as he can on the floor. He's on all fours, the T-shirt pulled up over his nose and mouth, crawling on all fours, dragging the Di Beradino along the floor, his face pressed against the floor, his cheek pushed into the carpeted floor. He's not coughing so much now, but his throat and his lungs are hurting and it scares him, this hurting.

He is heading towards the strip of incandescent mutable orange. Everything is black apart from this mutable strip. He is not in a room. He has lost all sense of this space as a room, of its dimensions, of dimension. It is a black void suspended in a black dimensionless universe. There is no world. There is only a strip of incandescent mutable orange. It is natural that he should head towards it.

It is strangely quiet. The shouting of the firemen, the sirens, the chopper noise all seem a long way off, muted by distance, on the other side of the black universe.

And now he's right up against the orange strip, which is huge now in the darkness, bigger than the darkness. He can feel the heat coming in through the orange strip. He feels that he could melt and merge with the orange strip. That his head will be the first thing to melt.

He reaches his free hand out blindly in front of him and comes up against a hot solid surface vertical in the darkness above the orange strip. He uses the vertical surface to help him get to his feet. His groping hand catches on something else solid protruding from the solid surface. Something it feels natural to grip and turn. And this gripping and turning enables him to pull the vertical surface towards him, opening the darkness, opening up a gap in the darkness that is filled with flames. He lifts the Di Beradino in front of his face, to protect his face from the force of the flames.

But even with the Di Beradino protecting him he is driven backwards by the heat of the flames. He doesn't turn round. He wants to face the flames. He wants to walk slowly backwards facing the flames.

The heel of one of his Nike Air Zoom Elites kicks against something. He looks down. There is light from outside now. He is at the balcony door and there is light flooding in from a nearby streetlamp. It is the bottom of the metal door frame he has kicked against. He sees a Pizza Hut logo on the floor of the balcony near the door frame. In the light from the nearby streetlamp he can see that it is a Pizza Hut pizza delivery box.

He steps out onto the balcony. He puts down the Di Beradino and picks up the Pizza Hut pizza delivery box. He can tell by looking at it that it's too big for the Di Beradino classic. He opens the Pizza Hut pizza delivery box and finds inside the little white plastic trestle that is used to keep the lid of the box from pressing down on the pizza. This is what he takes. This is what he puts inside the Di Beradino.

He looks around to make sure he is not seen. So it has come to this, he thinks as he places the Di Beradino classic on the high concrete balcony wall.

He hoists himself over. He grabs the Di Beradino. He runs and does not look back. He runs until he reaches the other side of the street, joining a cluster of onlookers. There's a guy holding a mobile phone aloft, pointing it towards the burning building, as if there is someone on the line who wants to talk to the burning building. A vague puzzlement causes Rob to look back, and the moment he chooses to look back an explosion booms in the burning roof space and a shooting jet of flame spirals up along the beam of the helicopter's searchlight. The helicopter tilts and sinks into the burning roof space and disappears behind the flames.

He cannot understand what he has seen. He looks for some kind of explanation in the faces of those watching. There is a communal gasp. Everyone gasps at the same time. The guy holding the mobile phone aloft lets his hand drop then raises it again.

49. The Nokia 6610i mobile phone

The phone has an integrated camera. She wasn't bothered about the integrated camera. She's never used it. Why would she want a camera? She can't see the point of having a camera in the phone. Bryan says she could use it to send him pictures of her tits. He looks at her slyly when he throws out smutty suggestions like that but she never takes the bait. These days she doesn't even deign to roll her eyes.

Yeah, you could send me pictures of your tits when I'm on the golf course. It might encourage me to get round quicker. And his eyes will be nervous and sly as he says it.

You take all the time you need, she might say. This is how their relationship works.

So it's Saturday morning and he's playing golf and she's in Brent Cross shopping for shoes and there's no way she's going to slip into the ladies to send him a photo of her tits. The thought makes her smile though. She will say that for Bryan. He can still make her smile. And there is something comfortable about the way their relationship works, his dogged desperate smuttiness with minimal encouragement from her.

But sometimes she can't help herself. I'm more interested in the vibrating function, she might say. Stuff like that sends him wild. Especially as she's so sparing with it.

Maybe one day she will surprise him. If she can work out how to use the integrated camera.

Classic design, high quality display, integrated camera, xHTML browser, FM radio, synchronize phone data on compatible PC, Java-enabled.

And now, as if the thought had set it off, the Nokia 6610i is vibrating in her bag. She has it on vibrate because she has never yet managed to find or create a ring tone she's happy with. And she thinks, That'll be Bryan. But as she takes it out of her bag she can see it's not his number, she doesn't recognise the number at all as she pushes the key to take the call.

Hello?

There is a beat before his voice, she knows his voice immediately.

Can you talk?

Yes, she says, because even though there is something comfortable about the way it works, her relationship with Bryan, there are times also when something comfortable is not what she wants.

Julia's gone to her mother's, he says.

How did you get my number?

I looked on the phone list. At work. Your mobile is listed on the phone list.

You could have asked me for it.

I'm sorry.

This feels a little creepy.

I know. I'm sorry. I was afraid.

This is borderline stalking.

I'll hang up now. And never call you again.

There's no need to do that.

There is a pause, then he says, Something else happened.

Oh yeah.

I haven't told anyone about it. I can hardly believe it. You know that helicopter that crashed. You must have heard.

Yes.

I was there.

Why are you telling me this shit?

You're the only one I tell. The only one I can tell. Julia knows about the body, about when I found the body. But I haven't told her about any of the others.

That's not answering my question.

I don't know. But there's something else.

What?

I can't tell you over the phone. There is a beat, then he says, Could we meet?

OK. The word comes out easily and it feels strangely lacking in import. She is looking at a pair of kitten heel sandals in the L.K. Bennett window. She is pretending that the L.K. Bennett kitten heels are all that matter in the world.

Where shall we meet? he says.

And she thinks perhaps after all she won't meet him. She'd rather spend the day in the L.K. Bennett store in Brent Cross trying on kitten heels. She'd rather spend the day on her own shopping for shoes. She's happy on her own shopping for shoes. She's happy shopping. It reminds her of the Saturdays she used to trail round after her Nan and she was never happier than then.

The last thing she wants is to meet him. She'd rather do anything in the world than meet him.

50. The Arofol Plus self seal postal bag

He returns the handset to its cradle. The cradle gives a little welcoming beep as it receives the handset. He has the Sony KV-20FV10 20" WEGA TV on BBC News 24. Muted. Very bad amateur footage of the helicopter crashing into the block of flats is repeated on a loop. He doesn't remember seeing anyone filming and then it comes to him. The guy holding the mobile phone aloft.

The helicopter crashing into the burning building has pushed the earthquake in Turkey off the lead slot in the news. Three men died, the helicopter crew. They show a still picture of the pilot holding his baby son. Miraculously, even the firemen on the aerial platforms escaped unharmed.

He has the objects spread out on the living room floor. His collection. The Snoopy ring binder. The Benjys napkin. The generic handkerchief. The NLHS badge. The Starbucks Coffee cardboard cup. And now the little white plastic trestle from the inside of the Pizza Hut pizza delivery box.

The letter to Mrs Emily Green is still inside the Di Beradino classic.

The entryphone buzzes. He goes into the hall to answer it.

Parcel, crackles the voice.

OK.

He bounds down the stairs and as he opens the door, the red Parcelforce van pulls off.

There's a bulging white jiffy bag on the doorstep, he would call it a jiffy bag, but as he picks it up, and it is satisfyingly heavy as he picks it up, he sees that the jiffy bag, as he would call it, is branded Arofol Plus self seal postal bag.

He reads his name on the label.

He's ripping it open as he takes the stairs. He's ripping apart the bulging Arofol Plus self seal postal bag and it isn't easy. The bubble wrap lining is rip-resistant. But he's impatient and his impatience makes him strong. He can't believe it has arrived so quickly, he is amazed, in fact, that it has arrived at all, and he's impatient now to see it.

As he closes the door to the flat he takes the weight out from the Arofol Plus self seal postal bag, all the weight is contained in a green onyx sphere the size of a grapefruit. The green onyx sphere comes out together with a compliments slip. But all he is interested in is the green onyx sphere the size of a grapefruit. So he drops the Arofol Plus self seal postal bag and he drops the compliments slip, though he is able to read the words Compliments of disaster.co.uk as it falls.

51. *The L.K. Bennett kitten heels*

He is standing high up above London. He is standing at the observation point on Primrose Hill. The whole of London is spread out in front of him. He imagines it engulfed in flames. He makes himself do this. It is chastening and necessary to do this. He knows how easy it is for things to become engulfed in flames. He looks for and finds the Telecom Tower. He imagines the Telecom Tower engulfed in flames.

He turns his back on London and sees her coming towards him. She is carrying an L.K. Bennett bag. She seems to receive his gaze like a blow.

Thank you for coming. He means it.

She shrugs. I was in the area.

Is that true?

She shakes her head without smiling. She seems smaller than he remembered her, slighter. More vulnerable. And looking at her face, at the beginnings of lines on her face, older too he would have to say.

So, she says, what's this all about? There is a nervous edge to her voice, as if the last thing she wants is an answer to that question.

One of the benches frees up. He nods towards it. They sit down. He goes straight into it.

I take things. When these things happen, these bad things, I take stuff. I always take something. You could call it a souvenir. But I think it's something more than that. I think it's a kind of insurance. I wanted to tell you because I thought you'd understand.

And you never told her?

No.

He reads satisfaction in her nod though she does not go so far as to smile.

Why not, I wonder.

I didn't think she'd understand.

And you thought I would?

Actually, I didn't tell her because. He breaks off and looks at the ground. I wanted to protect her.

That's a good one.

What do you mean?

She shrugs and says, Why do you think she needs protecting? Particularly.

I don't know. You'd have to meet her.

That's hardly likely.

When I'm with her. I can believe the world is not a totally fucked up place after all.

How sweet. And when you're with me?

He doesn't answer.

Sandra looks at her watch.

So, what now? That's the question, isn't it? That's the sixty four thousand dollar question.

What do you want to do?

Don't put all the responsibility onto me, matey.

I called you because I thought you'd understand. Because I thought I'd be able to tell you. About the taking.

And now you have. Hey, she says, suddenly bright. Do you want to look at my shoes? I find, when the world seems like a shitty place there is nothing quite like a pair of shoes to make things better. I suppose that sounds shallow? She is taking the shoe box out of the L.K. Bennett bag without waiting for his answer.

It's not shallow. I wouldn't say it's shallow.

She's showing him the shoes. They are pink and have bows and they seem as slight and vulnerable as she struck him a moment earlier.

Very pretty, he says.

Yes, she agrees. They're kitten heels, she adds. It's what she's famous for, Linda Bennett.

He tries to reward her with a smile. The kitten heels are delicate elegant things.

Listen, she says, as she re-boxes the L.K. Bennett kitten heels. All this stuff about taking things and stuff. It's definitely weird.

Yes.

It's a shame you're not a woman. He is nonplussed. She explains, You could just buy yourself a new pair of shoes instead.

He acknowledges the joke with a smile. Then serious again says, Before. You asked me how I feel when I'm with you. I suppose I feel the world is a fucked up place but I don't care.

She gasps. He is surprised to hear her gasp. What the fuck does that mean? she demands.

He shrugs. I think it means I'm in love with you.

Don't say that. How can you say that? She seems genuinely outraged. You don't even know me. You don't know me at all. And besides.

I shouldn't have said it.

Do you mean it?

I don't know.

If you mean it. Her mouth struggles with itself and puckers. You can't take it back.

I won't.

What about Julia? She puts the emphasis on Julia.

What about Julia? He puts the emphasis on about.

Do you love her?

I don't know. She wants to have children. I, I'm not sure.

You will. You will have children. You'll have children with her. She will be the mother of your children.

He puts his hands over his mouth and sighs through his fingers.

What the fuck do we do? he says.

There is one thing you haven't considered.

To his questioning glance she answers, Whether I'm in love with you.

Well? he can just about bring himself to ask.

She busies herself with putting the boxed up L.K. Bennett kitten heels back into the L.K. Bennett bag. She isn't smiling but she seems amused. Her eyebrows are raised in a way that suggests amusement. Then there is that same excessive fluttering of the eyelids that he noticed in the Feathers. When I was a little girl I loved my Nan, she says. I mean really loved her. I can't imagine ever loving anyone like that, she says. That was love, she says. This. This is playing.

52. The Faithfull Steel Shaft Claw Hammer 16oz

As he closes the door behind him there is a shape in the frosted glass panel and the door won't close and suddenly it is coming back at him and he is pushed back by the force of the door swinging towards him and there is someone else in the hall with him and it is no one he knows, it is a guy with the hood pulled up over his head and dark glasses on and his impression of the guy is that he is big.

And the hooded guy closes the door behind him. And to Rob's questions Yes? and Can I help you? the hooded guy's answer is to put his hand out and to push his hand into Rob's throat and to push Rob back by the throat so that his head bangs sharply against the wall. Another part of the hooded guy's answer is to turn Rob round and to yank his arm up his back, Christ it hurts though, and to whisper-hiss, Which is your gaff? in a way that is more menacing than if he screamed shut the fuck up at the top of his voice.

And Rob cannot help himself. Upstairs, he says.

So the hooded guy bundles Rob upstairs, all the time yanking that arm up his back so that Rob is screwing his face up to stop himself from crying. It would not do to cry.

Open it, the hooded guy whisper-gasps.

Rob gropes for the key with his left hand in the right pocket of his jeans.

As soon as he gets the door open, he feels himself impelled through it. Impelled. He is still a marketing man. The hooded guy slams the door behind them. He looks around, taking it all in, clenching and unclenching his jaw. His jaw is very square and he clenches and unclenches it a lot.

You got something of mine, he says. He's not whisper-hissing or whisper-gasping anymore. But his voice is a little breathless.

What? I don't know what you mean.

I was watching you.

Watching me? When?

Queen's Wood. You interrupted me.

The hooded guy nods once, tensely. He does that clenching and unclenching thing with his jaw and the tension shows in his neck too.

You? You killed him?

He was mine to kill.

What do you want?

What you took. It's mine.

Rob is confused as well as scared. But if this is what the guy wants he will give it to him. OK. All right. It's in there.

They go into the living room. The objects are still spread out on the floor. Rob picks up the NLHS lapel badge. He holds it out to the hooded guy. Much jaw clenching as the hooded guy takes the NLHS badge.

What's this? The hooded guy's voice speeds up and gets louder.

It's what I took. From the man. You killed.

I'm talking about the money. I saw you take his wallet. The hooded guy is shouting now.

Rob shakes his head. No, no. I looked at the wallet and then I put it back.

You what?

I put it back.

What are you? Mad?

I didn't want it. The money was no good to me. I wanted this. Or something. Anything. Just an object. From him.

The hooded guy looks at the badge in his hand. Then he looks at the other stuff on the floor.

What is this fucking sick shit?

It makes me feel safe.

The hooded guy clenches his fist around the badge and swings the fist back and Rob watches as the fist comes towards him and catches him square on the nose knocking him backwards. And in the pain and shock of it he cannot keep himself up. He sprawls backwards on the floor.

You feel safe now, Yuppie Boy?

The hooded guy pins the NLHS badge on his jacket. It is one of those soft hooded jackets, like a hooded tracksuit top.

Rob is lying on the floor, his cheek against the carpet. He's looking up at the hooded guy, thinking, You're not going to kill me. You don't want to kill me. I'd be dead already if you wanted to kill me. You knew I didn't take the money. You must have seen me put it back. If you were watching me. His nose is dripping blood and there is a heavy pain squatting in the middle of his face.

What's this other shit? the hooded guy says. He seems calmer now that he's hit Rob. Now that he knows Rob is in pain he can relax.

The file came from a girl, a student, who killed herself in front of me. The napkin was what another girl wiped her eyes on when her boyfriend dumped her. The handkerchief with the blood on it. There was an armed robbery. The blood came from the Security Guard. What else? The cardboard cup belonged to a homeless man. He gave it to me. He just gave it to me, for some reason. The, uhm, badge, that badge, as I said, it came from your friend. The white thing came from the inside of a pizza box I found inside that building that was hit by the helicopter that crashed. You know that helicopter that crashed. I was there when it happened.

The hooded guy crouches down, keeping his dark glasses pointed at Rob. He picks up the grapefruit-sized green onyx sphere.

The paperweight, says Rob. That arrived this morning. I bought that over the internet. A site called dangerousworld dot co dot uk. You can buy souvenirs off it. The paperweight, apparently, was recovered from Ground Zero.

The hooded guy clenches and unclenches his jaw and then starts laughing. Rob watches in some horror. This laughter is the worst thing he has witnessed yet. The hooded guy drops the paperweight to the floor. It lands with a heavy crack and rolls. It rolls towards Rob and he is able to catch it with one hand. He squeezes his hand around the green onyx sphere as if he expects it to yield to his grip like a soft toy.

You're fucking mad. I thought I was fucking mad but you're fucking mad.

Strange jagged sounds, Rob is producing strange jagged sounds, quaking sobs, and he can't control them.

The hooded guy clenches and unclenches his jaw.

I was thinking of going to Turkey, says Rob through the strange jagged sounds. To the earthquake. To see what I could get.

The hooded guy puts his hand inside his jacket and produces a metal hammer. It has a black rubber-sheathed grip and a slender metal shaft with a claw hammer head.

FAITHFULL CLAW HAMMER

A carpenters hammer with precision ground and hardened claws to withstand the most heavy nail pulling.

Securely fitted with steel shaft providing maximum leverage.

Each hammer is individually tested for weight tolerance, steel ingredients, crack testing, measured hardness, manufacturing processes, heat treatment and overall dimensions.

Head Weight. 16oz.

Do you want this?

What is it? The strange jagged sounds have stopped.

It's what I tapped him with.

Rob can only stare at the hammer.

You want it, don't you? You want it so much.

Rob nods.

The hooded guy brings the hammer down fast towards Rob's head. Rob closes his eyes. He hears the knock as the hammer hits the floor inches from his head.

Rob keeps his eyes closed. He can hear the hooded guy laughing.

You can have it, if you want it. But first you got to give me something.

Rob opens his eyes and looks at the hooded guy as he puts the hammer back inside his jacket. He is clenching and unclenching his jaw as he puts the hammer back inside his jacket.

You've got to give me the next one, says the hooded guy. He pats the bulge in his jacket caused by the Faithfull Steel Shaft Claw Hammer with the 16 ounce head.

53. The Nissan Bluebird 2.0GS

He got the car for two hundred sobs. Bargain. No doubt about it. The asking price was twice that. He had to lean on the twat who was selling it but that's par for the course.

Leaning is what he does.

There's a bit of rust under the sills. If the truth be known it's a fucking rust bucket but what do you expect. It goes like a dream though. Nothing wrong with the engine, that's the truth. Battery doesn't hold its charge but he can deal with that. Apart from that, it's fucking perfect. Smart car. He'd always wanted a Bluebird.

He doesn't bother with tax and insurance. It's a fucking joke in London. What do they think he is, made of money. He nicked a tax disk from this old beamer he saw. Tapped the window with the Old Faithfull. Sweet. That keeps the old bill from mithering him. They never look at the reg on it. When it runs out he'll nick another one. He's not made of money, is he?

Yuppie Boy is sitting next to him, looking like he's going to shit his pants or cry. There's a danger Yuppie Boy might scarper but he doesn't think he will. He has a feeling about Yuppie Boy. Yuppie Boy wants to be here. Yuppie Boy wants to see this through.

Yuppie Boy's got this letter he took from his briefcase. He's given him some address in Harrow. They're driving round Harrow looking for some address. Yuppie Boy has the A-Z.

Don't you piss about with me, he tells Yuppie Boy. You give me the next one, you take me there, you get me in, or it's you. And he puts his hand on Old Faithfull just to make sure Yuppie Boy understands.

Why does it have to be anyone? says Yuppie Boy.

That's funny. He has to laugh at that.

Don't ask fucking stupid questions, he tells Yuppie Boy. You know why. You know fucking why.

He can't believe this guy. He can't believe Yuppie Boy.

We're the same, he tells Yuppie Boy. You understand. I

understand you and you understand me.

It's true. He knows it's true. The way Yuppie Boy takes that shit, the reason he takes it. It's the same, it must be the same as the feeling when the Old Faithfull sinks in. You are at that moment in control. There are not many moments when you are in control of everything. Most of the time shit controls you. But at that moment you control shit. And if you are in control, you have no fear, you are afraid of nothing, you are not afraid.

You are the fear. You go to the heart of the fear and you become it.

It is lonely though, a lonely business.

He wonders if he can say any of this to Yuppie Boy. He wonders if he can be arsed.

Then suddenly Yuppie Boy is telling him to pull over. It's here, says Yuppie Boy. And there is the beginning of the feeling, knowing that soon it will begin.

54. The Yale P1037 door chain

She always keeps the door chain on. Of course. Even when Rod was alive, even when there was the two of them, they always kept the door chain on.

They are maisonettes but they have separate entrances. So she can put the door chain on. It doesn't inconvenience anyone. It isn't any trouble to Carla.

She will not open the door to anyone. Not unless she knows who it is. She has faith in the door chain. No one can get through the door chain. Carla explained it all to her. Carla has been wonderful. Who would have thought? All these years living in the same house, separate doors but the same house, and they hardly say a word to each other. It was all those earrings and studs she even has a stud through her cheek and the way she has her hair like a black woman though she's white. She has to admit she was put off. Frightened, yes. But now. Carla's been so wonderful. It just goes to show.

Don't let them in unless they show you ID, said Carla.

Emily opens the door as far as the Yale P1037 door chain will allow her.

- *Helps identify a caller before the door is fully released*
- *Surface fitted, providing ease of installation*
- *5 year guarantee*

There is a young man and his face is bruised and swollen which worries her but he's holding out a card in a plastic sleeve and the card has his picture on it and it's Diamond Life, it has what she recognises as the Diamond Life sign and the words Diamond Life and it also has the words SECURITY PASS. She can see all this.

Mrs Green?

Yes.

My name's Rob Saunders. I'm from Diamond Life. I need to talk to you about your policy.

They've already talked to me. They told me. It's no good.

There's been a mistake. On our part. If I could come in, I'll explain.

He has the card with his photo on it. It is him, though his face is not bruised and swollen in the photo. There is something else that troubles her about him too. She can't put her finger on it but it's something about his eyes.

What did you do to your nose? she says.

His hand comes up to cover his nose. An accident, he says. I was in an accident.

He's not dressed very smart, she points out, as if to some third person. Shouldn't he have a suit on or something? It's what she's thinking. Since Rod died she's taken to speaking her thoughts out loud.

It's Saturday, Mrs Green. I'm here on my own time. I wrote you a letter. I was going to send it to you. But I thought it would be better if I brought it round in person.

Carla is an artist. She has had exhibitions and been in the paper. That explains the studs and the hair. You should never judge people.

Yes, Mrs Green, he agrees.

He gets a letter out of his pocket and hands it through the opening.

She can see that it is addressed to her. She can see that it is in a Diamond Life envelope.

She opens the letter and reads.

Mrs Emily Green

42B Clevis Road

Harrow

HA2 5QS

Dear Mrs Green

May I apologise on behalf of Diamond Life for the obnoxious and insensitive manner in which your call concerning your flat roof problem was dealt with. We understand that now must be a very difficult time for you and, as a company, deeply regret adding to your distress in any way. Concerning your complaint, I would advise you to put the details in writing and send your letter to our Complaints Department at the address above. It is important to make a written complaint, as this begins the formal process of looking into your case. Please mark your envelope COMPLAINT. I am sorry you were not given this advice when you called.

If you are not satisfied with the way Diamond Life deals with your case, I would advise you to contact the Financial Ombudsman Service. Their number is 0845 080 1800.

If you require any further information, please do not hesitate to contact me on the number above.

Yours sincerely

Rob Saunders

Marketing

I've had people looking at it, she says. I've had quotes. I can't afford any of them.

It makes her scared and angry to talk of it.

Yes, Mrs Green. That's what I'm here for. We might be able to help you out. If I could see the quotes. I've been authorised.

She fumbles with the Yale P1037 door chain. There is still something about the young man that troubles her. It is the way he keeps looking to one side and shaking his head and it is the pleading look in his eyes as he shakes his head, as though he doesn't really want her to let him in.

But she has the chain off now and another man she realises there was a man there all the time to the side who he was looking at and shaking his head at and this man a man in darkglasses a man she didn't know was there has pushed past the young man with the bruised and swollen nose and she doesn't like this other man and suddenly the young man with the bruised and swollen nose raises his hand behind the head of the other man and she sees in the young man's hand something green and round and about the size of a grapefruit and he brings this thing whatever it is down on the head of the other man and there is a dreadful cracking sound and the man in darkglasses screams and the young man hits him again with the green grapefruit-sized thing and he hits him again and he keeps hitting him until the man in darkglasses sinks to his knees and he still keeps hitting him even then and he still keeps hitting him even when he is lying on the floor and there is blood soaking through his hood.

55. The i'coo Platon three wheeler

He's in Mothercare Brent Cross. He's in Mothercare with Julia and it's OK. He wants to be here. The strange thing is he finds himself taking pleasure even in being in Mothercare, waiting for the staff to make themselves visible.

He's taken the day off to be here. Strictly speaking, he took the day off to go with Julia to the Whittington for her 10 week scan. They paid the pound and got the printout. He was not prepared for the transaction, for the fact that he had to put the pound coin in a machine that gave him a token and he had to give the token to the ultrasound operator. Why you can't just give the money to the ultrasound operator. But he took pleasure even in that, even in the quaint token machine system. He is taking pleasure in everything now.

He has seen the life forming inside her, the smeary blur of grain that represents a life forming inside her. He saw it move and heard the heartbeat and now they have a printout.

So they decide to use the rest of the day to get some things for the baby. They will browse Mothercare and John Lewis, the John Lewis baby department and he has it in mind to stop off at Dixons, he has his eye on one of those Sony DVD cameras. You put the DVD directly in the camera. It seems to make sense to him. He's read about it and it seems to make sense. And besides, he likes the look of it, he has to admit that that comes into it, the liking of the look of it. He will make a record of the baby's life. He will film it growing up. He will be able to edit the film and put a soundtrack to it. And there will perhaps be a time in the future when the baby, though it won't be a baby any more, will use the camera for college projects.

At the Whittington they don't tell you whether it will be a boy or a girl. Julia says it's because some Indian families, there are a lot of Indian families in the area, and some Indian families don't want girls and will abort the foetus if it is a girl. He's not so sure about this. He thinks it's more to do with the fact that they like to get people in and out as quickly as possible, and

Christ it's hard enough finding the heart and the hands and checking all the other things they have to check. They don't want to get into that sexing thing, that would really slow things down. Besides, they could make a mistake. The penis of a ten week male foetus has to be hard to spot. They don't want the responsibility.

And it's OK, really he's OK with this. They will buy some things, there are always things to buy, especially now with the baby on the way, and they will have lunch at Waggamama's upstairs and it will be fine. The big picture is he's OK. Even to the extent that he doesn't get annoyed about the service aspect of being in Mothercare or about the token machine system at the Whittington.

They're looking at an i'coo Platon three wheeler and he's happy.

Sporty chic with innovative steering technology offering amazing comfort and superb handling, whatever the terrain

- *Suitable from birth*
- *Easy fold system*
- *Lightweight compact aluminum frame*
- *Self steering front wheel; lockable rear wheels*
- *Maximum manoeuvrability*
- *One - handed adjustable handle height*
- *Adjustable suspension system for a smooth journey whatever the terrain*
- *Hood with viewing window*
- *Removable bumper bar*
- *Easy on touch on/off brakes*
- *Easily removeable seat unit, can be rear or forward facing*
- *Chest pads for added comfort*
- *Adjustable back and foot rest*
- *Removeable washable seat cover*
- *Co-ordinating deluxe cosytoe included*
- *Large shopping basket*
- *12 month guarantee*

This is the coolest thing, says Julia.

She's right. It is cool. He never thought he would be able to think of a pram as being cool.

It says here it's all-terrain, he says, reading from the label.

There is a slight excitement to his happiness. A kind of enlargement and an awareness. Almost an eagerness. You can tell he's taking pleasure in everything now.

You could take him with you when you go running. Julia has got into the habit of speaking of the baby as a boy. Leaving that aside, she immediately regrets bringing up the running thing. She bites her lip to give a little public display of her regret. He knows she is thinking of Queen's Wood and what he found there and everything that came from it.

It's OK, he says. I'm OK. And he's smiling and nodding his head to reassure her. He really is OK.

They have talked about it. They have talked about the fact that he has killed a man. That the man he killed was a murderer who tracked him down because of something Rob took from a dead body he found in Queen's Wood. It was the badge that proved his story. In the end the badge was corroboration. Corroboration. He likes the word. He is a marketing man. Words, he has a sense of words. The widow of the dead guy in the wood confirmed that he had such a badge on his lapel. The letters turned out to stand for North London Historical Society. The police did not see the guy with the hammer as your typical member of the North London Historical Society. And there was forensic evidence too. Traces on the hammer linking it to no less than five murders including the dead man in Queen's Wood.

It is a strange kind of happiness comes in the aftermath of bludgeoning a man to death.

Of course he feels bad about the old lady. Did you have to put her through that? is a question he has been asked, by the police and by Julia. But the police accept there was an element of duress. Duress is a word that has been used. Duress. He likes the word.

He has sent her a cheque which he hopes she will accept.

In the meantime, he has to admit he is happy. Even with everything he put the old lady through, even knowing all that, even accepting all that she must have suffered at the bizarre and incomprehensible act she was forced to witness, and that coming so soon after the death of her beloved husband, even accepting all that, he is capable of being happy and it amazes him.

Things are working out at work too. He is settling into the job. They've worked their way through the long list and now they're onto chemistry meetings. There have been some changes. Number one being Tony is gone. It seemed his whole pub culture thing didn't fit in with Morello's vision for the future. As if I give a shit, being Tony's final word on everything, including Rob's promotion to his job as head of marketing. Coming newly promoted straight from Morello's office, he had to go past Tony's office and Tony was there still, clearing his desk to make way for Rob. He is to be one of the men who have offices now. Rob looked in, he felt he had to say something. I'm sorry, was what he said. As if I give a shit, came back from Tony. He did not explain why it should be he didn't give a shit.

And now the girl's with them, the Mothercare girl in the orange top, and she's taking them through the merits of the i'coo Platon three wheeler. Except she isn't really, she's carrying on a shouting conversation across the shopfloor with one of her colleagues about what time she takes her lunchbreak.

Rob can even take pleasure in this. He catches Julia's eye and smiles and she smiles back and there is something wonderful in her smile and in the end he realises it was the smile and the sense it gives him that after all the world is not a totally fucked up place, it was the smile that decided him. It is the smile that frees him.

Printed in Great Britain
by Amazon